The Icarus Boy

The Icarus Boy

Bill Regan

White River Press
Amherst, Massachusetts

ISBN: 978-1-935052-77-7
First published 2021 by White River Press
Amherst, Massachusetts • www.whiteriverpress.com

Cover image: *Icarus Falling*, mixed media © Bill Regan

Book design by Lufkin Graphic Designs
Norwich, Vermont • www.LufkinGraphics.com

Library of Congress Cataloging-in-Publication Data:

Names: Regan, Bill, 1937- author.
Title: The Icarus boy / Bill Regan.
Description: Amherst, Massachusetts : White River Press, 2021.
Identifiers: LCCN 2021042956 | ISBN 9781935052777 (paperback)
Subjects: LCGFT: Detective and mystery fiction. | Thrillers (Fiction)
Classification: LCC PS3618.E4464 I33 2021 | DDC 813/.6--dc23
LC record available at https://lccn.loc.gov/2021042956

CHAPTER 1

THE MOST PAINFUL EXPERIENCE OF MY LIFE—at that point, anyway—happened six years ago in mid-November, the time of year when darkness settles early over Boston. My wife and I were taking our daily after-dinner walk through Boston's Back Bay neighborhood, along the Charles River, across Hereford Street, and down a few blocks to our apartment on Marlborough Street, completing a two-mile loop.

In the spring, deep-pink magnolias create a striking contrast with the brick bowfront townhouses that line the streets of this nineteenth-century neighborhood. But in late autumn the flowers are a memory, and leaves no longer conceal the splayed skeletons of trees.

That evening, as usual, we talked as we walked, each sharing what our day had been like. She was finishing her internship in a city psychiatric center, and I was a homicide detective for Boston P.D. We talked only in generalities about our cases. I never discussed the gruesome details of my work, and she never revealed the names of her clients. The evening seemed no different than most others until we were within a block of our apartment. That was when she made her announcement.

"I don't want to be in the marriage anymore."

I stopped short, as if I had walked into a wall. I think I actually took a step back. My mouth hung open as I stared at her.

"What?"

"I'm sorry, but I don't want to be in the marriage anymore."

"*The* marriage? You mean our marriage?"

We had had trouble a year ago because of my long hours on the job, coupled with the pressure of Diane's finishing her master's degree. But we had worked that out—I thought.

She took a few steps toward our apartment. "Come on inside. We need to talk."

I couldn't move. "No, wait. You're telling me that you don't want to be married to me anymore?"

She nodded, her mouth now a tight line. "That's right."

I tried to suck air into a chest that suddenly felt as if it were filled with cement.

"We need to talk," she repeated.

"About what? It sounds like you've already made the decision."

"Why the marriage didn't work."

"Like, do an autopsy?"

Her face closed. "That's a terrible way to put it."

"I guess I've been a homicide cop too long."

"Nick, this isn't a murder."

"Then why does it feel like one?"

She reached out and took my arm. "Please, come inside."

At that moment, the idea of going into our apartment felt as if I'd be climbing into a coffin while she explained why she had to close the lid.

"Later," I said. I started down the street to where my car was parked.

I clocked more than a hundred miles that night—destinationless, aimless miles in the dark, while a storm raged in my head. I returned to our apartment after Diane was asleep and spent the first of many nights on the living room sofa.

We did talk, of course, the next day and the next, but she had reached her conclusions after lengthy analysis in her own mind, and she expected me to sit and listen without any messy emotional discussion. I realized that my autopsy analogy was not exactly accurate. All the autopsies I'd attended as a homicide detective were conducted on corpses. What Diane wanted, it seemed to me, was a vivisection. But I refused to stuff my emotions into a box so that she could feel comfortable. Two weeks later, I moved into a small top-floor walk-up across the river in Cambridge.

Boston got thumped by the first snowstorm of the year on Thanksgiving Day. It didn't matter much to me. The icy winds of a Boston winter could freeze me on the outside, but they would never be a match for the ice floe that had already encased my heart.

My father was an alcoholic, as is my brother. My father finally escaped his alcoholism when it killed him at the age of 64. As far as I know, my brother is still out there dancing to its destructive tune. Or he could be dead. I like to think I'd sense it if he left the planet, but I deal in facts, and the fact is, I haven't seen or spoken to him in eight years.

Because of them, I never considered using alcohol or drugs to ease the pain I went through that year. But on those first miserable winter nights, I'd sit in my crammed apartment in the dark, slipping the clip in and out of my automatic and think about eating a bullet.

Boston experienced a record number of murders in that dark season. Those homicides probably saved my own life, because pursuing the killers gave me a focus outside of my pain. I worked a lot of overtime and closed a lot of cases. I was relentless.

Our divorce went through in record time.

I haven't talked much about these events in the years since they happened. Partly because five months after my divorce became final, my life was forever changed by a registered letter, but mainly because reliving that time is like swallowing glass. I only mention it now because it proves something I believe I have always known deep in my gut but hadn't allowed to enter my consciousness: You can never, ever escape your past.

I held a three-foot tapered metal shaft in my gloved hand and stared at it. Getting there. I turned and clamped the shaft in a vise on my workbench, then removed my safety goggles to examine it some more.

Finally, I picked up a striker, lit my acetylene torch, adjusted the flame, and plopped a welding mask on my head as I began cutting irregular pieces out of one side of the metal with the flame.

About a year after my divorce, a letter arrived to inform me that my Uncle Frank had died, leaving me a substantial sum of money. I hadn't seen him for years, but when I was a kid, he had let me stay with him sometimes when my father was throwing furniture around our living room in a drunken fury. Frank had never married; he poured his time and energy into his business, a small manufacturing company that he eventually sold to a bigger one, netting him a staggering amount of money. Within a month of receiving my inheritance, I quit being a cop and moved to the Berkshire Hills in western Massachusetts. I found a house with a barn that I made over into a studio. I had always wanted to be an artist, and Uncle Frank had given me a chance to try.

I turned off the torch and removed my mask. As I loosened the metal from the vise, I enjoyed feeling its warmth through my asbestos glove. Placing it on an anvil, I slipped on my goggles and began pounding it with a heavy hammer.

As I struck the jagged metal, I experienced an odd but familiar mix of feelings. First, there was a sense of being detached and watching this object form before my eyes, almost as if I weren't shaping it with my blows. But under that was a subtle agitation deep in my body that felt almost sexual, or at least came from a parallel source. Its pulsing excitement filled my abdomen, then spread to my arms. I started working the steel faster, but with greater precision.

I was on it now, trying to form it until it gave me whatever it chose to share.

It's ironic that I experienced this process as close to sexual. Given my recent experiences with women, it was as close to sex as I'd probably get for a while. I seemed to meet people easily enough. The Berkshires are rural, but the little towns tucked throughout the hills have plenty of restaurants and pubs. The establishments that stay open during the long winters are havens for locals seeking the sight of another human face, a game of pool, or some friendly verbal sparring about sports or politics. I'd meet a woman, go on a couple of dates, and if we seemed to like each other, I'd get a spark of hope that maybe, this time, things would work out. But after being together for a while, we'd reach that point when it was time for more closeness—for intimacy—and I'd feel the old chill of that November evening years earlier and pull away. My chest would close in, and I'd feel a burning need to escape. I literally felt that if I didn't get into my car and go, I might die.

I looked at the battered metal shaft in my hand. Sculpting, even with its frustration and physical demands, was far easier than being in a relationship. And a hell of a lot less stressful than police work.

I walked to a large piece that lay tilted on its side. The base—a rough-cut, seven-foot-high oak pillar—was braced by thick blocks of wood anchored to the floor. The top consisted of an almost completed construction, a wooden ball bristling with irregular metal spikes. The jagged shaft I'd been making was a meant to be a spike in this brutal medusa. The ball, spikes included, was about five feet in diameter. It rested on a pair of metal sawhorses, and as a safety backup, I had lashed a thick rope around the ball and run the rope through a ceiling pulley and tied it to a heavy cleat on one of the studio's vertical support beams.

I pulled off my gloves and slumped into a scarred captain's chair. The spiked sculpture reminded me of the Medieval maces I had first seen in a museum. The image had never left me. It also conjured the violence in which I had been both a witness and a participant in my years as a police officer. Even though I had been off the job for almost five years, grisly images of homicides still smoldered in my brain. Mostly, they appeared in dreams—eerie revisitings of murders I had investigated.

A six-foot mirror leaning against the wall across the studio framed me slumped in my chair. I scratched the silver-gray hair I'd had since I was twenty-two and noted the dark circles under my eyes.

"You look like hammered dog shit," I said to my reflection.

The wall clock informed me that it was almost one in the morning. Ten hours had passed since I had entered the studio in bright daylight. I pulled myself out of the chair, killed the lights, and trudged upstairs to my bedroom.

CHAPTER 2

I COULDN'T REMEMBER when I had been here before. Along the dim corridor, stains and peeling paint marred the walls between battered doors. Empty bottles and syringes littered the torn linoleum floor. A naked bulb hanging at the far end of the hall provided a meager light that failed to dispel the darkness surrounding me.

I moved slowly, trying to avoid crunching the glass vials. I was here to arrest someone. The problem was, I didn't know who—or even if they were male or female, young or old. But I did know that whoever the perp was lived behind one of these numberless doors.

Sweat pooled in the hollow of my throat and streamed down my chest and belly. As I fumbled with the buttons of my soaking shirt, panic spread through me like fire, and I ripped the shirt open. The sound of buttons popping echoed in the corridor like tiny gunshots.

Suddenly the light went out, leaving me in total darkness. I heard someone moving in the hallway. A bottle skittered across the floor. A glass syringe splintered underfoot.

I reached for my gun, but my fingers found only an empty holster. Frantic, I pawed my pockets. No gun.

My heart banged against my chest. I turned to run and slammed into a wall in the dark. Somewhere behind one of the doors, I heard the distant ringing of a phone.

The persistent ringing brought me back to my darkened bedroom. I was soaked with sweat, tangled in my blanket and sheet. The ringing came from my own landline on the bedside table. I groped for the receiver.

"Yeah," I mumbled.

Silence hummed on the line. Still stunned by sleep, I wondered if the phone had actually rung. My clock read 2:35 a.m. I'd been asleep a little more than an hour.

"Hello," I said.

The silence held. I was about to hang up when I heard a woman's voice.

"Nick."

A jolt of adrenaline sat me up, wide-awake.

"It's Diane," she said. "I'm sorry to call so late, but . . ."

I couldn't speak.

"I know you probably don't want to hear from me."

That had been true since I found out she had divorced me not because "the marriage" wasn't working, but because she was involved with her supervisor.

"Nick?" she said.

I took a long, deep breath before I spoke.

"How did you find me?"

"I called your precinct and talked to Ellen Frost. She said you weren't with the police anymore and were living in Rimfield." Ellen worked with teen offenders and taught a course that Diane had taken when she working on her master's degree.

"Yeah."

"She heard that your ship had come in—whatever that means. What have you been doing?"

"Unloading it," I snapped.

She went silent.

"What do you want, Diane?" I carried the cordless receiver out of the bedroom and sat on a wooden bench by the railing overlooking the living room. My breathing was almost as constricted as it had been on that November day six years ago. Her call felt like an invasion.

And yet.

"Nick, I never would have bothered you except that I'm in trouble. You're the only person I can think of who might know what to do. I'm really sorry to intrude after all this time."

"What about your guy, the shrink?"

"He—he dumped me. Two years ago." She swallowed audibly.

A jolt of savage glee ran through me. I took another breath and shook it off. "So, Diane, what do you want?"

She sighed. "I'm not sure, but I think a man is following me, and it could have to do with Jimmy—a client of mine, a young college kid. He's in a lot of trouble with some pretty bad people. Less than an hour ago someone called, breathed into the phone, then hung up."

"Did you see the guy you think is following you?"

"I've seen him twice now—a tall, curly-haired man."

"Have you talked to the police?"

"No. I don't see how I can do that without getting Jimmy involved," she said.

"Does the kid know any curly-headed men?"

"I don't know. He missed his last appointment."

"Diane, are you sure this isn't a coincidence? That the guy with the curly hair couldn't have just been in the same place that you were for some other reason?"

I heard her let out a shaky breath.

"You know how you used to talk about your intuition?" she said. "Well, that's how I feel—that something is very wrong." She stopped, drew in a deep breath. "Look, Nick—could I meet you somewhere?"

That question put me on my feet. I began to pace the balcony.

"It's been a long damn time, Diane. There must be someone else."

"Please, Nick. I'm scared."

I shook my head but said nothing.

"Please," she continued.

I went downstairs to the kitchen and started a pot of coffee. Sleep was out of the question tonight. I wanted to refuse, but an older yearning shouldered my resentment aside. "All right," I said finally. "Where do you live?"

"In Waltham. I bought a little house."

"Give me the address," I said.

She gave it to me, then said. "I'm sorry, but I feel like I need to get out of here. I'm really creeped out."

I had never heard Diane sound afraid. "Okay," I said. "Meet me at the Charlton plaza on the Mass. Pike. It's a little west of Worcester, about halfway between us. Everything's going to be closed, but we can meet in the parking lot. What are you driving?"

"A red Honda Civic."

I put her on speaker while I pulled on a sweatshirt and jeans. "This troubled kid, his name's Jimmy?" I asked.

She hesitated as she always did about identifying her clients. "His last name is Ryerson," she said finally. "Jimmy Ryerson."

That didn't ring any bells.

"His stepfather is a big-shot developer in the city, Jonathan Price. Have you heard of him?"

I froze. Price had been suspected of ties to organized crime for years, but no one could ever prove it. Suddenly, Diane's fears had a basis.

"Yeah, I've heard of him," I said, snatching my car keys and a jacket. "It'll take me about 90 minutes to get to the Charlton plaza," I said. "And I have one condition. Call

911 before you leave and tell them you have an intruder and are leaving the house for your own safety."

"But I'm not sure—"

"You're sure enough to call me. Make the call. And get the hell out of there. I'm leaving now," I said.

CHAPTER 3

AFTER I DRESSED, I went into my den and walked to a 30-by-40-inch painting hanging on the wall. I took my key ring from my pocket and inserted a small key into a lock on the side of the canvas. The painting, mounted on a door, swung open to reveal a rack that held twelve handguns, some of them antique. I stored rifles and shotguns behind another painting on the first floor, next to the gym.

I removed a flat-black Sig Sauer in a belt holster and slipped the holstered gun onto my belt on my left hip, butt forward. After closing and locking the concealed door, I went down to the kitchen, filled a thermos with coffee and slipped on the jacket.

I glanced around the kitchen, trying to slow my racing thoughts. It angered me that I was this excited by the prospect of seeing Diane again. What made me the angriest was the fact that I had fooled myself into thinking I was beyond her emotional reach. Yet one phone call and here I was, running out my door.

I grabbed the thermos and stepped onto my porch. I stood there in the dark, pulling in lungsful of the still, cold May mountain air. When I felt calmer, I locked the door and jogged to my car. The black Porsche 914 convertible was my biggest extravagance, made possible by becoming suddenly wealthy and investing well. It was exactly 3:00 a.m. when I kicked the engine over and headed for the Mass Pike.

I knew Diane must have a hard time picturing me as anything but a cop. Years of working as a detective had conditioned me to be always watchful, whether or not I was on the clock. No matter where Diane and I went, my eyes swept the scene, seeing things most civilians missed. She hated it, because it took me out of whatever was happening in the moment and dragged the dark ugliness of the criminal world—my world—into our life together.

At the end of our marriage, she recalled an example of my "copness," as she called it. We were with her friends Cindy and James, sitting on a bench in the Boston Public Garden. It was early June, and we were enjoying the warm, sunny day and the beds of flowers that attracted hundreds of pedestrians. Diane leaned her head on my shoulder and said something like, "What a glorious day."

I agreed, but then added, "It's too bad those two jerks are going to spoil it by fighting."

She lifted her head. "Where?"

"Right there." I pointed at two well-dressed men having an animated conversation under a willow tree by the decorative pond.

"What, those two guys?" James said. "No way."

I shrugged and said nothing. No more than two minutes later, one man pushed the other, and then they were rolling on the ground, pummeling each other.

Diane, Cindy and James turned in unison and stared at me.

I shrugged again. "After a while, you learn to read people."

That ability to read the tells, as gamblers call them, was invaluable to a cop on the street, but to Diane it was a reminder of the violent world I inhabited. I had been a homicide detective when she met me and a homicide detective when she left me. It was the only life I knew, so I had never considered any other work, even for her sake.

"Nick," she told me the day after her November announcement during our walk. "You're a wonderful guy, but you're always on alert. I can't stand it when those gray eyes of yours suddenly go dark and hard. It scares me."

To ask me to stop being a cop was like me asking her to stop believing that all the adolescent scumbags she worked with were worth saving. We both had way too much hard-wiring to easily change. I know I had said that to her, probably more than once.

But our beliefs about our identities are not always as sacrosanct as we think they are. When the unexpected chance to walk away from police work had presented itself, I had grabbed it. And for five years I had not looked back.

I asked my phone to dial Diane's number, and it rang nearly 12 times before I gave up. I tried her again 15 minutes later, and again 15 minutes after that. By 4:00, I was approaching the exit for the Charlton plaza, a half-hour earlier than planned. I rolled into the parking lot, where a line of tractor-trailers was parked along the side of the empty lot under the street lights, motors chugging to keep the heaters on. I topped up the gas in my tank and parked, gazing at the sky as the darkness leached away. But after phoning Diane for about the tenth time without a response, I couldn't sit there another minute.

I hit the pike with a heavy foot and made it to Waltham within half an hour. At 5:15, traffic was not an issue as I threaded my way through the downtown to the residential neighborhood, following my phone's turn-by-turn directions. As I slowed to make the turn onto Diane's street, a dark Jeep Wagoneer was pulling out. Its driver, a lantern-jawed guy wearing a knit cap, glanced at me as he drove past. Probably headed for a seven-to-three shift.

Diane's house turned out to be a small white Cape set back from the street on a narrow lot. A white fence bordered the sidewalk with flower beds running along its length. Well, Diane had the flowers she used to talk about.

I parked in the silent street and closed the door of the Porsche as softly as I could, but it sounded like a bomb. I walked to her gate and paused. No lights were on inside or outside of the house—strange, since she knew the police were coming. I took the flagstone path to the front step. I pressed the doorbell and heard it echo in the house. No lights went on, no sound of movement. I pressed the bell again and held it. Nothing. A tickle of fear danced along my spine.

I opened the screen and knocked sharply on the wooden door. No response, and it was locked. The tickle was turning into an icy probe. I left the front door, crossed the lawn and walked down the narrow driveway that cut between the Cape and a split-level next door.

My breath caught when I spotted a red Honda Civic parked in a small open garage at the end of her drive. Diane had not left the house. All my senses went on high alert.

I climbed three cement steps and cupped my hands to peer through her back door into the kitchen. A table stood against the opposite wall with a straight-back chair at either end. On the floor, near one of the chairs, lay what appeared to be two envelopes, torn open, and several sheets of paper scattered around them. Diane was a neat freak. She would never leave a mess like that. I unzipped my coat and unsnapped my holster.

The back door was locked as well, so I left the steps and backed into the yard to check the windows. The last window on the first floor was open, a plastic milk crate on the ground under it. I climbed onto it and looked cautiously into what seemed to be a spare bedroom. Its door was open, and I could see into a hall beyond.

I scrambled through the window, landing on the floor next to the bed. Now the automatic was in my hand. Aside from my own breathing, I could hear no other sounds. I found the hall empty and followed it toward the kitchen. I checked an empty bathroom on the right. No sign of Diane in the kitchen, but as I stepped over the paper I had seen from the back door, I noticed that more opened mail had been tossed into the sink. The dining room showed no signs of disruption. Neither did the living room. A staircase ran up the far wall to what I guessed would be Diane's bedroom. I took it two steps at a time.

A door at the top of the stairs was closed. I gripped the knob and pushed it open. No sound or movement here either, but two pairs of socks, rolled in balls, one red, one black, lay on the floor with a pink silk blouse crumpled between them.

The second floor was one large room running the length of the house, except for a bathroom facing the stairs. Her bedroom took up the end to my right. Her office, with computer, file cabinets, and bookcases, filled the area to my left. Three skylights were spaced at intervals along the back of the house, illuminating the chaos of the room in cold morning light. It had been torn apart, clothes and files strewn everywhere. File drawers hung open. The desk drawers had all been yanked out and dumped onto the floor. In the bedroom, her dresser had been emptied. A walk-in closet was littered with jackets, skirts, blouses and shoes. Even the futon bed had been disemboweled.

And still no sign of Diane.

I went back downstairs cautiously, suddenly aware of sweat running down my chest and back. Whoever had trashed the house appeared to be gone, but I knew better than to trust appearances. The only place left was the basement. The thought sickened me. In the home invasions I had investigated, when residents were taken to the basement, it was always for the worst purposes.

The cellar door opened off the kitchen. I pulled the door open and stepped back. I glanced down the stairs, then squatted and listened. No sound, but I tensed at the smell of cigarette smoke. Diane was a militant non-smoker. As I sniffed, I recognized other smells mixed with the burnt tobacco. Their unpleasantly familiar odor made me want to cry. Burnt flesh, and mixed with that, the odor of cordite. A gun had been fired. I fought off a tremor and started down the stairs.

As I descended to what I knew I would find, I could feel myself begin to slip into cold, objective, unemotional armor, just as I had always done on the job. I had learned that skill years before to protect myself from the horrors I encountered. Now, even after five years, it was involuntary. I was back in the shit.

And there she was, her back toward me, sagging against the ropes that held her to a wooden chair. I knew she was dead before I reached her.

Her head hung against her left shoulder. The belt of her bathrobe was draped across her right shoulder. I holstered my gun and instinctively put my hands behind me as a reminder to not touch anything. I slowly circled her body, but then the armor cracked. I squatted next to her and, as if I were afraid I would wake her, I tipped her head up and looked into her face. Her eyes were partially open, staring into a dimension far from this ugly basement.

She had been burned repeatedly across her face—her nose, her lips, even around her eyes. Burn marks traced down the front of her neck, disappearing into the folds of her robe. I had no desire to see what had been done to her breasts. Tears began to blur my eyes. I swiped at them with the back of my hand and took deep breaths.

But even in death, even after all this, she was still beautiful. I lowered her head and stood up, my hands behind me again. I had to get it together, pay attention.

The cause of death seemed to be a bullet wound behind her right ear. The hair around the wound was matted with blood. There was no exit wound. Possibly a small caliber—.22 or .32. I had seen no neighbors out looking around, which indicated a silencer.

Before I called the police, I needed to be the investigating officer, to keep busy—to avoid the terrible realization that I had found her and lost her again all at once.

There were no butts on the floor, although the smell of tobacco, the size of the burns, and the ashes that clung to the back of her shoulder and nestled in her lap told me a cigarette had been used. Whoever killed her had swept the floor, cleaned up everything. A professional, and there would probably be no incriminating prints anywhere.

The son of a bitch must have grabbed her right after we talked. He had worked in a gruesomely effective way, and obviously enjoyed causing pain. I flashed on the Jeep that had passed me as I arrived. The man in the knit cap with the lantern jaw. I wondered if the hat had concealed curly hair—and if I had been that close to Diane's killer.

I took a deep breath and turned back to her. Not that long ago, she had been my wife, my lover. I had the impulse to say some sort of good-bye and to tell her that I would do what I could to avenge this, but I remained silent. I never spoke to the dead—not to the vics of my crime scenes, not even to my mother, and certainly not to my father. The real Diane was gone: only her shell remained, drained of life, and forever beyond my voice or my reach.

But not so the curly-headed man.

CHAPTER 4

I stood in the kitchen, trying to think like a cop. Diane's mail had been searched, so it made sense that the guy wanted something that had come in the mail—maybe something from that kid she'd been counseling. Because this was now a crime scene, I didn't want to contaminate it by searching the house more thoroughly. Plus, the way it had been torn apart led me to believe that, if there had been anything there, Diane's killer would have found it. The fact that he had tortured her probably meant that he hadn't. Whether she'd told him where to look was unknowable. My only logical alternative was finding the office where Diane met with her clients.

I carefully walked through the house until I spotted her purse lying in a corner of her home office, probably tossed there by the perp. Using my handkerchief, I lifted it by the base and dumped its contents onto the floor. A small rectangular metal case slid to the wall. I opened it and found her business cards with her office address. I pocketed one, wiped the case, placed it on the floor, and went downstairs. A quick search of the kitchen turned up her car keys, plus four others. Hoping that one of the keys opened her office, I pocketed the bunch.

Doing this was in violation of everything I had been taught. At that moment, with Diane's body in the basement, I didn't care.

If the perp had any brains, he'd have found the same cards. But because the purse hadn't been dumped, and the keys were still here, maybe he didn't know she had an office. Or perhaps he had found a spare set and was on his way there now. If I hurried, there was an outside chance of arriving while he was still there, or even before he found the place. Either way, he was mine.

But in order for that to happen I couldn't get tied up with the police. I'd have to leave Diane in the basement.

I left by the front door as quickly and as unobtrusively as possible. The neighborhood was still quiet. Three houses down, I saw a van backing out of its driveway. It turned and drove off in the opposite direction. I climbed into my car and got out of there.

Her office was in Arlington. The morning traffic snarl turned the twenty-minute drive into a forty-minute crawl. I had exhausted my extensive vocabulary of expletives by the time I reached her office.

It was one of several in a pale-gray, two-story rectangular structure sitting on the corner of Arlington's main drag. I left the car with Diane's keys and tried the exterior door. It was locked, and the second key I tried opened it. A registry in the foyer informed me that Diane's office was on the second floor. I slipped my gun out and took the stairs to a corridor lined with offices. Her name hung on the last door on the left, across from a waiting area with chairs and magazines. Another key fit that lock and, for the first time, I entered Diane's professional world.

I holstered my gun when I saw no sign of an intruder. Her large office was tasteful, neat, and orderly, like Diane. Facing the door were two leather chairs, each with its own side table. A box of tissues sat on the table next to what I took to be the client's seat. A couch, a desk, and a file cabinet lined the far wall. Large plants were strategically placed to soften the austerity of the space. Nonconfrontational art added to the air of comfort. For some reason, perhaps because it had never been part of our lives together, I felt more like an intruder here than at her house. Maybe because I hadn't been invited. I shook off these thoughts and looked around.

Using my handkerchief, as I had on the doors at her home, I went through the desk. Nothing there appeared to be related to the cause of her death, which I assumed to be the Ryerson kid. I turned to the file cabinet, which, as I expected, was locked. Since I had seen no key in her desk, I tried a small key on her ring in the lock. It worked. I pulled the top drawer open and started searching for Ryerson's file. And I found it.

It was fat, containing Diane's handwritten notes on Ryerson for the past two years. I sank into the client's chair and started reading.

CHAPTER 5

WHEN JIMMY RYERSON had made his first appointment
with Diane, he was a freshman at Barnum College, a
private school outside of Boston. Diane had diagnosed
Jimmy with situational depression and referred him to a
psychopharmacologist for a mild antidepressant. Ryerson
had spent two weeks in Diane's office talking about his
family and his life at college before he got around to what
was really eating at him—his belief that his step-father,
Jonathan Price, had murdered John Ryerson, Jimmy's
father. Price and John Ryerson had been partners in real-
estate development. The business had flourished, even
though the elder Ryerson had a history of heavy drinking.
The main reason for the business' success, according to
Jimmy, was that his father had been sober for four years.
During this new and brighter chapter in his father's life,
the family's money problems had ended, along with his
parents' fights. That is, until his father had disappeared,
two and a half years ago.

Jimmy's mother had called the police and hired a
private investigator, all to no avail. After six months,
Jimmy's mother filed for divorce, telling Jimmy that
his father had obviously left them for good. Jimmy had

argued on his father's behalf until his mother married
Jonathan Price about a year later. At that point, Jimmy
had withdrawn from the family and begun to follow Dad
into the bottle.

I stopped reading. The Price scenario sounded
painfully close to my own family history, except that
my dad hadn't disappeared, despite my earnest wishes
that he would. I hadn't followed him into the bottle, but
my brother had. There was nothing in Diane's notes to
reveal why Jimmy thought his father had been murdered,
except that he believed that Price was connected to the
mob. And to back up his suspicions, in his last session
with Diane Jimmy had mentioned some names—names
that were well known to Boston P.D.'s organized crime
unit: Frankie Fallon and Carmine Antonelli.

Now the story unfolding in the notes had my attention.
How in hell did Jimmy Ryerson get those names?

A month ago, Jimmy had started coming to therapy
hung over and surly. Two weeks ago, he showed up
visibly drunk and proclaimed that he finally "had the
goods" on Price and was planning to "burn him down."
The notes contained no explanation of what the "goods"
were or how he planned to take Price down. Diane had
ended the session early and managed to persuade Jimmy
to leave his keys and go home by cab. That had been the
last time she'd seen or heard from him.

I put down Diane's notes again, sat back in her chair,
and closed my eyes. If the Ryerson kid was messing with
Frankie Fallon, the kid was facing a short future. After the
death of his kingpin father, Fallon had seized control of
organized crime in parts of greater Boston. Any question
of the younger Fallon's ability to retain power had been
quickly settled when the bodies of three of his rivals
turned up—in pieces—along the beaches of Boston's

North Shore. The cops had quite a time putting them all together.

Carmine "Snake" Antonelli was Fallon's right-hand man, as smart and ruthless as his boss was. I had never met Frankie, but Snake and I had a history. We grew up together in the same neighborhood and had started socking each other almost on day one.

The notes provided me with a record of Jimmy Ryerson's moods and motives up until two weeks ago. If he had really gone after Price and Fallon, the kid was on a dangerous journey. Being a drunk, not to mention young and inexperienced, practically guaranteed he would fail to pull off whatever scheme he had hatched.

I stood up and checked my watch—7:26 a.m. People would be arriving soon to open their offices. I needed to finish up here and figure out my next move. There was one remaining key on Diane's ring, small and flimsy like the key to the file cabinet. I circled the room slowly and couldn't find a lock for it. Maybe a post office box? I tapped myself on the forehead. I had walked past a bank of mailboxes in the entryway.

I locked Diane's office door behind me and hurried downstairs. The last key fit the door to her mailbox. I opened it, took out a bundle of envelopes and thumbed through them. Bills, flyers, and one personal letter with the return address of a woman whose name had not been mentioned in Jimmy Ryerson's file.

"Shit," I muttered, as I stuffed the envelopes back and closed the door. I had no idea where the Ryerson kid might be. Barnum College was my only link to him. I pocketed the keys and started to open the outer door when a flash of yellow on the floor caught my eye.

I stooped and picked it up. It was a postal notice addressed to Diane, telling her that a package too large for the mail drop was being held for her at the local post office. I crammed it into my pocket and opened the door. A tall man with a gray goatee was climbing the steps. I turned away from him as we passed each other. I didn't want a witness. Outside the post office I called the Waltham police, gave them Diane's address, told them there had been a killing, and then hung up when the dispatcher started asking questions. I hoped that they would be gentle with her body.

I took a baseball cap from behind my car seat, hung a pair of sunglasses on my nose, and walked into the post office. Three people stood in line in front of the counter while a red-faced man waited on them. He was abrupt, bordering on rude, as he moved the customers along. When I reached him, I placed the slip on the counter. As the clerk snatched it up, another employee, a young kid with long hair, wandered out from another part of the building.

"Hey, Ray," the long-haired kid said.

The older man turned, my slip in his hand, said, "You're late again," and stalked off.

The kid looked after him, shook his head, and unlocked a drawer farther down the counter. I turned away from him. A few minutes later, Ray returned. He flipped a large manila envelope on the counter in front of me, then turned to the kid. "You gotta get here when you're supposed to," he complained.

"Geez, man—it was only five minutes . . ."

Ray locked his drawer, then walked by him, glaring. "They're my five minutes."

As I left, I couldn't help smiling. These two were too busy squabbling to remember me.

In my car, I opened the envelope, which was reinforced with a piece of cardboard. DO NOT BEND was hand-lettered on the front and back. Inside were three 8×10 black-and-white photographs.

In the first photo, two men were talking outdoors, with the ocean in the background. The shot was a little grainy, but I recognized Fallon, his heavy, square build topped with a round head covered in tight, wavy black hair. A ridiculous pencil-thin mustache grew under his small, straight nose. I had always thought Fallon looked like a two-bit actor auditioning for a B-level gangster flick.

The other man in the photo was Jonathan Price, rumored to be Fallon's expert money launderer. When I worked for Boston P.D., the organized crime detectives who tailed Price had never actually seen him with Fallon, a fact that frequently left them frustrated and pissed off. The FBI was also keen on connecting Price with Fallon. Even though the feds had devoted endless hours to taping all Fallon's calls on all of his known phones, they hadn't managed to record any conversations between them. Clearly, Price and Fallon spoke over disposable cell phones. Burners, in crime lingo. The only evidence that Price and Fallon worked together was the testimony of one of Frankie's former soldiers, who was subsequently placed in witness protection.

Price's vanity license plate further irritated his investigators: *Le Renard*—French for "the fox." Anyone running this fox to ground would make a career on it.

Back when I was on the force, Art Fowler, my old partner, and I were sitting in a car on another surveillance one day when Price had happened to walk by, and Fowler pointed him out to me. Price was a little taller than my six feet, with reddish hair cut short on the sides. A forelock repeatedly slipped down over his left eye, giving him a youthful look that belied his actual age, which was mid-forties. He was stocky, bordering on fat. This softness, coupled with petulant rosebud lips, reminded me of some of the entitled Ivy League types I had met. Only his cold, narrow-eyed gaze betrayed his character and the double world he inhabited—a shadow world of false respectability. He sat in his beautiful home—where Jimmy Ryerson had lived until leaving for college—and entertained wealthy guests while some pretty bad people did him ugly favors.

Price's value to Fallon lay in his ability to successfully launder gang money, probably through offshore accounts. However Price managed it, the IRS and the Justice Department had been frustrated in their attempts to get indictments against Fallon.

Jonathan Price, his petulant lips frozen in mid-word, was in the second shot with Fallon again. Deep in conversation, they were coming out of what looked like the side door of a warehouse.

But in the third photograph, Price was talking to someone I had never seen—a slim man shorter than Price, probably five-ten or so. A neat dresser in a conservative suit, the unknown man wore his hair sort, almost a crew cut, on a square head. Sunglasses sat on a long, slightly hooked nose. Both men leaned against what looked like a Ford. Another car, clearly a Mercedes, was parked in the background by a tree. They were in a field or a park in the country, with no buildings in view. Price was gesturing, his right hand extended and pointing.

I placed the photos on the passenger seat and looked into the envelope again. A folded piece of lined yellow paper had been pushed to the bottom. I shook it out, then unfolded a note scrawled in an adolescent longhand:

Diane, I'm sorry to send this to you, but I don't know what else to do. I'm in trouble. Two of these pictures I took show my lousy stepfather with a Boston gangster. I guess that's why I'm in so much trouble. My stupid stepfather likes to pretend he's a big-shot businessman instead of a crook.

I don't know who the guy is in the third shot, but Jonathan drove all over town before he finally met the guy. He even doubled back a couple of times, like he wanted to be sure he wasn't followed. He's always telling me how smart he is, but I was riding my motorcycle and he never even saw me. How smart is that?

Anyway, please either give these to my friend Robbie Atkinson in room 305 in North Hall at Barnum College, or hide them somewhere yourself. I can't go to Barnum again because a scary-looking goon who works for my stepfather almost caught me there a couple of days ago. He was going to hurt me, maybe even kill me. They don't know you, so you'll be safe.

It's really important that these photographs be kept somewhere safe. If anything happens to me, give them to the police. I'll call you later.

                                    Thank you.

I put the letter and photographs into the envelope and started the Porsche. Well, Ryerson had been seriously wrong on one point: They, whoever they were, did know who Diane was, and where she lived. They had murdered her to get these photographs, and the only reason they had failed was because Diane had not yet picked up the post-office notice. Now they would probably turn their attention to this Atkinson kid. If they knew about Diane, it was a good bet they knew about him. Jimmy Ryerson had definitely overestimated his abilities. But what was so damaging about these shots that Price and Fallon would kill to get them back?

I pulled into traffic and headed for Barnum College.

CHAPTER 6

BARNUM COLLEGE SAT ON A HILL. The hill's elevation and the abundance of trees and shrubs on campus masked the densely urban surroundings. North Hall, Robbie Atkinson's dorm, stood about a hundred yards from the college gate on a drive that looped through the campus. I found it easily and lucked into a parking space right in front of it. The dormitory was a three-story Gothic building with spires on each end and a prominent blue door at the center of its brick facade.

I checked my watch—9:20 a.m. Atkinson might be in his room or he might be gone for several hours. The dorm's blue front door was locked, so I waited until a student came out, then caught the door before it swung shut and stepped into a foyer lined with bulletin boards. Sheets of paper advertising upcoming school functions, apartment vacancies, requests for rides, and other urgencies of college life cluttered the boards' surfaces. A worn easy chair, missing its left front leg and propped on a block of wood, featured a cardboard sign that read Adopt Me. Uncle Sam had paid for some college courses for me before my inheritance, and I felt oddly reassured that, despite the advent of computers and email, people still slapped notes up on bulletin boards.

The whole dorm was quiet. To the right, stairs descended from the foyer into the basement. I walked past them into the main corridor, which ran the length of the building, with staircases at each end. I noted the order of the room numbers on the first floor and climbed the stairs closest to 105. Room 305 was at the top on my left. I knocked. Silence. I tried the door, found it unlocked, pushed it open, and stepped into a spacious living room with doors on the sides.

"Robbie?" I called out.

I heard a mumble and movement from behind one of the doors. It swung open and a young man, his long hair matted from sleep, stuck his head out.

"Are you Robbie Atkinson?" I asked. The not-too-buff young man, wearing only a pair of boxers, scratched his head and squinted at me. "What time is it?"

I glanced at my watch again. "Nine-fifty-five. Are you . . ."

"Holy shit!" The young man yelped and ducked back into his room, leaving the door open.

I walked to the door, listening to the boy move around and swear to himself. Peering in, I saw two bunk beds against the opposite wall of the narrow room. Two bureaus lined the door wall, and a closet faced the large front window with its shade drawn. The young man had pulled on a pair of tattered jeans and was struggling into a wrinkled shirt. I leaned against the doorframe.

"Why do I think you're not Robbie Atkinson?"

"Cuz I'm not," the boy answered, fumbling with his last button. "I'm Todd Dawson, Robbie's roommate."

"Any idea when Robbie'll be back?"

"Probably an hour or so," Dawson said, ramming his feet into an old pair of topsiders. He squeezed past me. "Sorry, I gotta go. If I miss this class again, he'll flunk me."

He grabbed a notebook off a cluttered desk and stopped by the door, running his fingers through his tangled hair.

"You can wait if you want." He started out the door, then stopped again. "Thanks for waking me up, mister. You really saved my ass." And he was gone.

I stood in the room and looked around. Two tall windows faced out onto the main drive, with two desks standing side by side beneath them. One was piled with books and notebooks. Papers tumbled off the desk and into an open drawer. Todd Dawson's, no doubt. It looked as disheveled and confused as he did.

The other desk was the opposite, with books and notebooks stacked neatly against the wall. A coffee cup held pens and pencils. Pinned on the wall above this desk were three photos. In one, an older couple sat behind three adolescents, two boys and a girl. One of the boys wore sunglasses and looked irritated, as if he couldn't wait to leave. In another photo, the same young man, a little older and not irritated, stood with his arm around the shoulder of a taller young man who looked about the same age. The taller guy had his hair pulled back in a ponytail, the end of which hung over his shoulder. A lovely young woman smiled out of the third photo—a graduation portrait, by the look of it.

I checked the time: forty-five minutes until Atkinson would be back—maybe. I sat on the couch, felt a deep fatigue settle in my body, then stood up and headed downstairs. Leaving the building, I asked a passing student where I could get a cup of coffee.

The coffee shop was a short distance from North Hall. I bought a large coffee and returned to the dorm. I watched students hurry across campus. They looked so young, with so much compromise and disappointment ahead of them. *Damn, you really are tired.* I got into the dorm the same way I had before and returned to Atkinson's room. I left the door open while I sat on the couch and sipped the coffee. I was finishing it when students started returning to the dorm, yelling, running upstairs. Five minutes later, the shorter boy from the photos, now wearing a blue-plaid shirt and wheat-colored jeans, walked into the room, calling, "Hey, Todd, you forget class again?" He stopped when he saw me. A flash of fear was replaced almost immediately by indignation. "Who the hell . . . ?" he said, then turned and called, "Todd, you here?"

"Todd went to class," I said, "He said I could wait here."

Atkinson stayed where he was, five feet into the room. "Who are you? What do you want?"

I gestured to a chair. "My name is Nick Magill. I'm here about Jimmy Ryerson. Sit down—please."

Atkinson, a wiry kid who couldn't have weighed 150 pounds, said, "You stand up. This is my room."

Gutsy, I thought, as I pulled myself off the couch. "You bet," I said. "But I still need to talk to you about Jimmy."

The earlier fear crept back into his eyes, but he blinked it away. "There's no Jimmy here."

"Sure there is," I said, taking a gamble and pointing to the photograph of the two young men with their arms around each other. "He's right there in the picture with you. Now please, let's sit down and talk."

Atkinson said nothing, but he perched on the arm of an easy chair facing me.

"Do you know Diane Zeolla?" I asked.

Atkinson frowned. "I've never met her."

"But you know of her? Jimmy's mentioned her?"

"Are you a cop, Mr. Magill?"

I closed the door and sat down on the couch again. "Used to be. Now I live in the Berkshires and play at being an artist. I guess you could say that Diane Zeolla and Jimmy sent me to see you."

CHAPTER 7

I WAS TOO TIRED TO DANCE with this kid, so I decided to trust my instincts that he was mature enough to handle what I had to say. I told him about Diane's call, how I had found her, and enough of what happened to make Atkinson turn a little green.

"It's vital that you tell me where Jimmy is," I said when I wrapped up.

Atkinson was silent. The fingers of his right hand drummed on his thigh. Finally, he said, "Look, Mr. Magill, you seem like you're telling the truth, but how do I know you really want to help Jimmy? Maybe you're just bullshitting me so you can hurt him, like the other guy who tried to grab him."

"What do you know about that?"

"Not much. Just that a big ugly dude with curly hair was waiting for him outside the dorm. The guy grabbed Jimmy by the arm and tried to pull him into a car. Jimmy stomped the guy's foot and twisted away, then ran like hell."

The curly-headed man. "Sounds like the same guy who . . . who killed Diane. Back to your question. You don't know me, and you have no reason to trust me, but

I'm here to warn you. One friend of Jimmy's is dead, and I think you're in danger too. So either trust me or call the police, but don't do nothing."

Confusion and fear reappeared in Atkinson's face. "Shit," he said.

"Yeah," I said. "And if Diane's killer knows you . . ." I let it trail off.

"He does," Atkinson whispered, swallowing hard. His eyes met mine. "Jimmy called, told me the guy was waiting for him right outside. So he must know where I live." His eyes flitted to the front windows as he spoke.

"It happened in front of the dorm?" I asked.

"Yeah, at night," the boy said, pulling himself together. "Jimmy was bringing me some stuff to hold onto, and this guy grabbed him. When Jimmy got away, the guy shot at him."

Ryerson hadn't mentioned any shooting to Diane. "Did anyone report the gunshots?"

"I don't think so. Jimmy said they didn't make any noise, like those silencers in the movies."

I leaned forward. "Look, Robbie, you're in danger. You need to get out of here, go someplace safer. You're his next logical choice."

Atkinson shook his head. "I can't. I've got finals next week. I've got to study."

"Good, Robbie, we'll put that in your obituary: 'Died with a book in his hand.'"

Atkinson opened his mouth, then closed it. "Can we get some coffee?" he asked finally.

"Sure," I said. "Let's walk, but let's keep our eyes open."

"It's daytime," Atkinson said. "He won't do anything in broad daylight, will he?"

"Let's be careful, just in case," I repeated.

Atkinson nodded. We left the room and started downstairs. Atkinson asked, "So, Todd was here when you got here?"

"Yeah. About an hour ago."

"That's Todd," Atkinson said shaking his head. "Stay up all night, sleep all day."

"It does seem kind of difficult to sleep through a ten o'clock class. Must take a lot of planning."

Atkinson laughed. "Todd never planned anything in his life." Then he added, "But he's a great guy, really thoughtful. He'll do anything for you."

"If he wakes up in time," I said.

We were both chuckling when we stepped outside. As we started down the incline to the campus steps, I noticed a black Jeep Wagoneer illegally parked by a hydrant on the street. Its driver was staring at us. He had a long face with a heavy jaw. The top of his head was in shadow, so I couldn't see his hair. But this was the Wagoneer I'd seen pulling out of Diane's street.

I took Atkinson's arm and stepped between him and the street, unzipping my coat. "Did Jimmy say what kind of a vehicle the guy who attacked him was driving?"

"Some kind of SUV, dark colored," Atkinson said.

As I stared at the Wagoneer, the driver cut the wheel and pulled away from the curb. When he sped past, I caught a glimpse of curly hair. A blast of adrenaline propelled my hand to my gun as I pivoted to track the retreating car, but I didn't draw the weapon from its holster. Within seconds, the Wagoneer reached the end of the drive, started to turn left, stopped, then lurched to the right. I straightened and turned back to Atkinson, whose eyes were bouncing from me to where the speeding car had been.

"What's . . . who was that?" he stammered.

"I don't know, but the driver had curly hair and a long face. And I saw the same kind of vehicle pulling out of Diane Zeolla's street last night."

Darkness flooded Atkinson's eyes. He opened his mouth but did not speak.

I took a small sketchpad from my coat pocket and jotted down the Wagoneer's license number. It was probably stolen.

When I looked up, Robbie Atkinson was staring at my open coat. The butt of my gun was visible. I closed and zipped the jacket.

"Oh, God," he whispered. "This is really happening, isn't it?"

I started down the hill. "Let's go get that coffee," I said.

CHAPTER 8

W̶E̶ ̶S̶A̶T̶ ̶A̶T̶ ̶A̶ ̶C̶O̶R̶N̶E̶R̶ ̶T̶A̶B̶L̶E̶ in the Commons. As we were getting coffee, I realized I hadn't eaten anything since lunch yesterday, so I ordered a cheeseburger. Robbie Atkinson had lost his appetite. We sat in silence for a few minutes while I devoured the burger and Atkinson sipped his coffee. He couldn't keep his eyes off the door to the street. Finally, I leaned toward him.

"Chances are he won't wander in here," I said.

He managed to squeeze out a faint smile. "That obvious, huh?"

"Yup. Let's get down to it, Robbie. Where's Jimmy?"

Atkinson stared at his cup as if some vital information floated in there. He frowned, then sipped some more coffee.

"Well?" I asked.

"I don't know . . . exactly."

Exactly? An anger that I had managed to push away since arriving on the Barnum campus tightened its grip on my neck and shoulders. I ran my hand over my face and took a breath. "What does that mean, Robbie?"

He sighed, his eyes finally climbing out of the cup. "I think he's on the Cape—probably in Hyannis." He finally looked at me and plunged on. "I think that because Jimmy's drinking again. See, he's an alcoholic, like his dad—his real dad. He had trouble in high school and stopped drinking before he came to Barnum. He went to Alcoholics Anonymous until he decided to try to drink once in a while. I guess he was handling it pretty well until that close call outside my dorm. Since then he's been drunk a lot."

"He started getting drunk after this guy almost killed him?"

"I guess it was the pressure," Atkinson said, a little defensively.

Another surge of anger hit me. "More like stupidity," I blurted.

Atkinson straightened in his chair and gave a snort of disgust. "You sound like my father."

I held up my hand. "Sorry, I didn't sleep last night. So Jimmy's back to drinking, and you think he might be in Hyannis. Do you know where?"

"I don't know," he said with a frown. "Maybe this isn't a good idea."

I kept my voice low and even. "Telling me is a good idea because Jimmy's out of control, and he's panicked. That psycho in the Jeep will kill him when he finds him. That's a stone fact. They will also kill anyone who they think knows where he is—after they torture the information out of them. You're in exactly the same spot as Diane was, because they believe you have information they want."

I paused to let my words register, then continued. "So it doesn't matter if I fuck up and sound like your father, your mother, or your goddamned Aunt Lucy. What matters is that we get you to a safe place and that we find Jimmy before he winds up breathing the same air as Diane."

For a second, I saw the boy's chin quiver. But then his face closed like a fist, and he suddenly slammed his hand on the table, making his coffee cup jump. People turned to look at us. "All right—fuck this," he said. "I told Jimmy he was screwing himself by trying to get his stepfather. I'm not willing to die for his bullshit."

I nodded but said nothing.

"You know Jimmy's dad disappeared a few years ago, right?"

I nodded again.

"Jimmy's mother said that he was probably out on a bender, and maybe he got hurt or ran off with another woman. But Jimmy got the idea his stepfather killed his father, or had him killed, you know, like in the mafia." Atkinson looked at me with a bleak expression. "Jimmy was, like, possessed," he continued. "He couldn't leave it alone. I think he told Diane because of how nice she was, easy to talk to."

I nodded. She was—had been.

Atkinson went on, caught in the story. "Diane was like an anchor for him, more than school. Jimmy was—is— an English major. Anyway, he was able to hang in okay until April, when he took the pictures. The fact that he got them seemed to push him over the edge. He started talking about rescuing his mother, even though I pointed out that she didn't want to be rescued. He stopped going to A.A. meetings and started drinking again. After he took those photos, I guess his drinking got even worse, at least until that guy attacked him." He stopped and raised his eyebrows. "I told you what he was like after that."

"Where was Jimmy's mother during all this?"

"Probably shopping," the boy said bitterly. "Despite what Jimmy says, I don't think she cares about anything— or anyone else—as long as she can buy stuff." He shook his head. "Except for Diane, Jimmy was all alone."

"He had you," I said.

Atkinson shook his head. "Jimmy's my friend, but I'm a college student. I didn't know what to do to help him."

"Why would he be in Hyannis?"

"It's just a guess, but that's where he first got sober. He went to a two-week program at a hospital, then to one of those houses that alcoholics go to in the community."

"A half-way house."

"Yeah, that's it. He made friends in A.A. down there."

"So you think he's getting sober on the Cape again?"

Atkinson hesitated. "Maybe, but that's also where he did his worst drinking the summer before he got sober. So he has some drinking buddies down there, too."

I finished my coffee. "Do you remember any of the A.A. friends he made, any names he mentioned?"

He smiled, nodding "He really liked a nurse he met while he was at the hospital. I can't remember the name—the something-view Treatment Center, I think. Sea or Lake or something like that. She worked there, and she was also sober. Jimmy saw her at A.A. meetings after he got out of the hospital. I think her name was Jean."

"Was he involved with her?"

"You mean like, dating?"

I nodded.

"No, no. He said she was pretty, but she was a lot older. They were just friends, like Diane."

"How much older was she?" I asked.

Atkinson thought for a second. "Quite a lot. She was way in her thirties."

"That old?" I groaned.

Atkinson grinned, actually blushing a little. "You know what I mean."

"Did Jimmy tell you her last name?"

"I don't think he even knew it. They don't use last names in A.A."

We walked back to the dorm. So now I had some things to work with: the nurse's first name, and the city where Jimmy got treated for alcoholism. Hyannis wasn't a big city, so this could be enough to go on. Nothing certain, but enough.

I considered staying with Robbie Atkinson in case the curly-headed man showed up again. But since Jimmy Ryerson was the key to all this, I decided to get Atkinson into a safe place, find Ryerson, and take him to the police, who could protect him. I had to admit that I was also more than a little curious to find out what he knew—and what he could prove—about Jonathan Price.

But under it all, I knew that if I had Ryerson, the man who had tortured and killed Diane would come to me. And that was what I really wanted.

My biggest obstacles in this pursuit were not tactical, but emotional. In a word, rage. During my years with the police, I had shot two men in self-defense, not killing either one of them. When I left the force I thought I had left this kind of violence behind, except for the dark dreams that still haunted me at night. But it had popped out again just now, over coffee with Atkinson. I had handled it, but at my core, I was shaken by its power. It had driven me to break all the rules I had lived by for years.

Now, walking across the Barnum campus, I knew that when the time came, I would not be able to control the anger Diane's death had triggered. I would find the curly-haired man, and I would kill him.

While I was getting honest with myself, Robbie Atkinson was talking about how he really needed to stay at school because of next week's finals. We went back and forth about asking to take his exams online, but someone had recently hacked the system to change grades, and the prof was going back to in-person tests, no exceptions. I held firm, so Atkinson called a friend who lived off campus and arranged to stay there on the couch. He assured me that six other people lived in the building, and his friend's room was in the attic, the safest place of all.

I voiced my opinion that to be anywhere near campus was unsafe, but I reluctantly agreed that it was safer than staying in the dorm. And what the hell, I wasn't this kid's father. I couldn't force him to stay with his parents in Connecticut.

No Wagoneer was in sight when we arrived at North Hall, but I knew that didn't mean much. Curly could have ditched that and stolen another car by now. I scanned the drive, checked the cars within view of the dorm. No one in any of them. Maybe we could get clear of campus before the scumbag came back.

The kid was a champion packer. We had loaded the Porsche within fifteen minutes. Before leaving, he insisted on going back in to leave a note for his roommate, so Todd wouldn't worry. Within minutes, he came out on the run and squeezed into the front seat, piling books onto his lap. I checked the area again, saw no one suspicious, and started the car. I pulled out slowly, checking for a tail. I saw no one. Once we left the campus and entered the urban traffic, it became more difficult. I spotted one Wagoneer, but it was red.

Atkinson's friend's house was a Victorian mongrel, added onto and altered over the years. It sat in a short cul-de-sac a half-mile from the campus. The interior was larger than it appeared from the street. Atkinson led the way up a steep, creaking staircase from the second-floor hallway. At the head of the stairs, he turned to me. "This is it, my new home."

"These stairs sound like they're ready to collapse," I said.

"Like a haunted house," he answered as he opened the door.

The room was more of an oversized dormer with windows on three walls. I opened the largest window, which faced the door, and fresh air began to cut the stuffiness of the room. Through the window screen, I could see the roof sloping down into the branches of a large maple tree next to the building. I helped pile the boy's clothes and books on the spare bunk, and then leaned against a wooden storage crate.

"Okay, Robbie, you say your friends will be home later."

When he nodded, I continued, "Remember, if you insist on taking finals, do not—repeat, do not—go alone. When you're on campus or around campus, or even here, as far as I'm concerned, you're in danger. Having other people with you will diminish that risk but not take it away. Do you understand?"

Atkinson shrugged and nodded again. "Yeah, I suppose so, but I feel like I'm being babysat."

"Look," I said, "Do you want more details of how Diane looked and what exactly that animal did to her?"

"God, no," he yelped. "But—"

"But?" I cut him off, the rage stirring. "I was a homicide detective for Boston P.D. I have seen atrocious violence perpetrated on human bodies of all ages—that's right, babies, old men, everybody. Nobody sees it coming, or they wouldn't have been there."

Atkinson put his hands up. "Okay, okay, I won't go on campus alone. Shit, I won't go anywhere alone."

I took a deep breath. "Now you're getting it."

We finished putting things away in silence, then, as I was pulling my jacket on, the boy said, "You know, I wonder what's wrong with adults—not you particularly, except you get angry pretty easily—but our so-called grownup parents? My folks included. They all seem so screwed up. Jimmy's father is a drunk. His mother's greedy and shallow. His stepfather's a crook and maybe worse." He shook his head. "People just seem to grow up and become fools, thieves, liars, jerks, and worse. They've screwed up the economy, the environment—you name it. This country's a mess. The whole world hates us. Why does this keep happening?"

I shrugged. "I don't know, Robbie. It just seems to repeat with every generation. All I can say is, don't look now, but you're almost one of those grownups yourself."

"I know," He dropped onto the bed. "And it really pisses me off."

CHAPTER 9

AFTER I LEFT ATKINSON, I decided to call my old Boston
P.D. partner, Art Fowler. We had remained friends after
I retired. I knew he would help me, as long as I kept my
plans for Curly to myself.

The call went to voicemail. Probably he was out
on a homicide, so I left him a short message: Call me
when you're free. Before heading for the Cape, I stopped
at a copy center and had the guy at the machine fiddle
with the darks and lights until he came up with decent
reproductions of Ryerson's photos. The copies weren't
as clear as the originals, but good enough to fax to
Art. I hoped he would recognize the man in the third
photograph. Regardless, he would be in a position to
contact the Barnum campus police to set up protection
for Robbie Atkinson. They'd listen if Art told them that a
murderer might be loose on their campus.

It was almost 3:00 when I swung onto I-93 south
and headed for Hyannis. My fatigue was agitated by a
caffeine buzz. I found some classical music on the radio
and let it smooth out some of my ragged edges as I drove.
Unfortunately, the music couldn't erase the memories of
seeing Diane's mutilated body, the latest horrific image

in a stack of older ones accumulated during my cop years. The image I was grateful to be spared was of Diane lying naked and vulnerable on a tipped metal table. I had witnessed enough autopsies to know their indignities. It infuriated me to think of her being subjected to the coroner's knife while he droned impersonally into a hanging microphone. All Diane had done was treat a troubled kid. And while she was being sliced open like a goddamned halibut, the curly-headed man was still out there, getting ready to hurt someone else.

The Ryerson kid was doomed if he kept on drinking while the monster who had killed his therapist hunted him. Not to mention stupid. Otherwise, how did he think he could pressure and outfox the fox himself—Le Renard—and the other pros who specialized in extortion and murder? But hell, the kid was a drunk, and drunks seemed to possess an infinite capacity for arrogance.

My father, Patrick, had always been drunk, or so it seemed. I knew that "always" wasn't completely accurate, but "usually" certainly covered it. "Always" did apply to all holidays and family gatherings and important functions such as weddings, graduations, and funerals. On Fridays, most of the kids at school were happy that the weekend was almost here. My younger brother, Darren, and I did not share their feelings. Only Jim Beam knew what good old Dad would do with two days off, but we knew we needed to avoid crossing his path—and attracting his wrath.

Darren is two years younger than I am, so I tried to look out for him. But when he was ten or eleven, he started smoking cigarettes. A year later, he was stealing our father's beers, even though he got a beating whenever Dad caught him. Darren didn't seem to care. On his fourteenth birthday, I caught him smoking pot and took it away from him. But it was a waste of energy, because

Darren had already drifted into the world of booze and drugs. By the time I joined the military after high school, his addiction was taking him out of the house for days at a time. In his junior year, it took him out of school for good. I had no idea where he was now. Probably taking Dad's place on a barstool somewhere.

Drunks. I could never understand them. Put a damn bottle in the middle of the railroad tracks with an express train bearing down, and some drunk would take a shot at getting it. I could picture the bastard sprawled on the tracks, every bone in his body shattered, and still lifting his head to ask, "Did the bottle break?"

And alkies are liars. Whenever my father opened his mouth to speak, he spewed an endless stream of lies. I finally figured out that most of the time he was mainly lying to himself. Dad would tell us that he was going out to have "a little liquid refreshment," like it was a glass of water, or like he was going to have just one cocktail. Like he was the social drinker he apparently wanted to be.

Except that social drinkers don't pass out on the front steps, or piss themselves at a Christmas party, or puke at a wedding banquet. And they don't usually unleash their personal demons on everyone they supposedly love. My father wasn't often physically abusive, but the phrase "verbal abuse" could have been coined with Pat Magill in mind. As plastered as he got, he managed to remember every mistake that any member of his family had ever made. And used it like a club. My mother, always a timid person, couldn't or wouldn't defend us. He bullied and shamed her at every opportunity, and over time she faded to near invisibility in our household.

Finally, when I was seventeen and Darren fifteen, alcohol took our father out of the family and into the street. My mother's eldest brother, Uncle Frank, forced the issue after he and their two other siblings staged an intervention at our house. Their mistake was that Dad was already drunk, and he puffed himself up with righteous anger and bellowed at them to leave his property. I still remember my mother's cringing face. The next day Uncle Frank came back right after work and told Dad to pack up. My uncle then drove Dad to the Boston YMCA, where he could rent a room. Dad protested, but he hadn't had a drink since the previous day's binge and probably felt like hammered dog shit. Whatever the reason, he saw the set of Uncle Frank's jaw and caved. My mother and Darren and I watched the scene from the kitchen doorway.

For years, I had prayed that Dad would leave us. So when he moved out, I expected Ma and Darren to share my relief. But Darren just clammed up and wallowed in more drugs and alcohol than ever. My mother slid into a depression. No matter what I said or did, I couldn't pull her out of it.

Two days after my high school graduation, I joined the army and trained for the military police. I had no idea then why I chose to become an MP. All I seemed to do was hassle with drunks. It was a drag in the States and ten times worse when I got to the Philippines, which rolled out a chemical red carpet for U.S. soldiers. They sampled the whole damned smorgasbord and got into every imaginable kind of trouble—knifings, rapes, brawls, vehicle accidents. It was a drag, but I stayed with it, and I learned a lot about being a cop.

My father died three days after I arrived in Manila, and I didn't even try to get back for the funeral, which my mother pulled together. I felt guilty later, especially after Ma wrote me about how hard it had been for her, and how Darren had shown up drunk and embarrassed her. A year later, I did go back for her funeral. It was painful to see her in the coffin, her face pinched and sad under the mortuary makeup. She would have been devastated if she had known that Darren didn't show up at all, drunk or sober. A neighbor told me that, six months after the funeral, Darren had come around, looking rough, like he'd been living on the street. When he learned that Ma had died, Darren vanished again.

The squawk of my cell phone pulled me back onto Route 3 just as I was passing an exit for Plymouth. It was Robbie Atkinson, calling from a train en route to his parents' home in Connecticut. And he had quite a story a story to tell me.

CHAPTER 10

Aᴛᴋɪɴsᴏɴ's sᴛᴏʀʏ went something like this:

Lacking a closet in his new attic digs, he pinned up a makeshift clothesline across the room and hung his shirts there on hangers. He didn't like blocking the air from the large window that I had opened over the roof but knew it was just temporary. Meanwhile, he stacked his books and looked around the room, thinking yes, the place would work. And also agreeing that I was right—this plan was smarter than sitting in his dorm room, where that crazy guy could just walk through the door. He decided to make a pot of coffee before studying. While it was brewing, he sat on the bed and checked email on his phone. Then he heard the stairs groan outside the door.

He looked at his phone—3:05 in the afternoon. None of the housemates was supposed to be home until after 6:00. My description of what happened to Diane Zeolla roared through his mind as he stared at the door four feet away. He heard nothing and started to dismiss the sound as a product of nerves. But then the doorknob turned, the door started to open, and a strange male voice yelled, "He-e-e-r-r-e's Johnny!"

What Atkinson did next amazed him. As the door swung into the room, he leapt up and slammed his weight against it. As the door crashed shut, he heard the intruder fall back onto the stairs. Robbie turned, ran full-tilt through his hanging clothes, dove through the window screen and landed on the roof. He rolled, kicking the screen away from him, and slid into the branches of a big tree. He grabbed hold of a branch and scrambled—almost tumbled—to the ground. When he landed, he glanced up, didn't see anyone, and ran like hell.

I had to smile. Gutsy kid, obviously proud of his instinctive self-defense moves. But not so proud that he was staying for finals. He took the first cab he saw to the train station, deciding as he climbed in to take make-up exams and get his belongings later. I asked him to call his friends and the campus police to let everyone know about the attack. He said he would, thanked me for warning him and promised to call me if he heard from Ryerson.

I praised Atkinson for his courage, his smarts, and his sane decision before I hung up. But I wasn't happy. Curly must have followed us, and that worried me. There was a time when I would have spotted a tail within the first two blocks. If Atkinson hadn't reacted the way he had, he'd be taped to a chair, either dead or wishing he were. I needed to regain my old skills quickly, or else I'd wouldn't be able to stop Curly before he found another victim.

CHAPTER 11

THREE MILES AFTER I HAD CROSSED the Cape Cod Canal, Art Fowler called, his ex-smoker's gravelly voice dramatized by the phone. "Nick, I'm glad you called. I was going to call you. It's about your ex-wife. Diane's been . . ."

"I know," I interrupted.

"Oh. I'm real sorry, Nick."

"Thanks, Art."

"How did you find out?"

I was silent.

"Nick?"

"It's a long story. I'll tell you when we have more time."

"Is that why you called?"

I paused again, weighing how much I wanted to tell him, now that Atkinson was safe. My hesitation was not because I didn't trust him but because he was still a cop, and I didn't want to put him in an untenable position.

"Art, I can't talk about this right now, but I can exchange some information with you."

"What information? Nick, what the hell is going on?"

"Did you get the photos I faxed you?"

"What photos?"

"Check the fax machine and call me back."

Five minutes later the cell chirped again.

"Where the hell did you get these shots of Price and Fallon? Our pals on the Organized Crime Task Force are going to soil themselves when they see these."

"Serves them right," I said. "If I were a member of the OCTF, I'd be embarrassed as hell to find out that some college kid got those shots when none of my highly trained hotshots could even come close."

"What kid?"

"The one I am currently to find. His name's Jimmy Ryerson. He's gone missing from Barnum College."

"Holy shit. Why're you the one who's looking? Do you know this kid?"

"No," I said. "I'm just doing a favor for a friend."

"What friend?"

"That's not important."

"Hey, Nick. How long've we known each other?"

"A long time," I said.

"Then do me a favor, buddy. Don't bullshit me."

I sighed. "Ryerson was a client of Diane's. I think those photographs are why she was murdered. Ryerson mailed them to her, but she hadn't picked them up yet. Unfortunately, the sadist who got to her didn't know that."

"How do you know . . .? Damn, Magill, you're the one who found her, aren't you? You were the anonymous caller."

"I can't answer that without one of us getting our nuts caught in a wringer."

"You crazy bastard. Why are you in this? After what she did to . . ."

"I'm in it, Art. I'm not sure why, either. But the why of it doesn't really matter. There's a curly-haired psycho out there. I think he killed Diane to find Ryerson as well as to get his hands on the photos. He needs to be stopped."

"By the law, buddy. By the law."

I said nothing.

"Nick?"

"Will you help me?"

I could hear him swearing under his breath. Then he was quiet. Finally, he said, "This isn't in my jurisdiction, Nick. The staties are running it."

"All I need is information. Give the photographs to the state cop running the show. Maybe they'll help. Tell him you got an anonymous call about Ryerson."

"If I do that, both of us could get screwed."

"And I'll bet they won't kiss us first."

That squeezed a chuckle out of him. "You always were a little nuts," he said. "What do you need?"

I described the man I had seen in the Wagoneer. "Any thoughts about who he could be?"

"You sure Fallon's involved in this?"

"Yeah. Ryerson's stepfather is Jonathan Price."

"Damn," Art said. "That ties it all together. I don't know all of Fallon's people, but I can talk to Eddie Bemis. He's spent a lot of time with the task force on Fallon."

"Great," I said. "I have the plate on a car he was driving."

"You've seen this guy? Where?"

I told him.

"Yeah, that makes him for Diane's death, but the car and the plate are probably both stolen."

"I know."

He sighed. "Okay. Let me see what I can dig up. Where are you now?"

"Following a lead into Hyannis."

"For Christ's sake, be careful. You're way out there on a limb. Don't fuck yourself."

"Don't worry," I said. "I'm not that limber."

CHAPTER 12

In Hyannis I found a parking space on Main Street that got good cell reception and Googled the name of the woman Atkinson had given me, Jean McKinnon. There was a J. McKinnon on Main Street in Centerville, about two miles away. I set the map app and drove to her address.

McKinnon lived in a small cottage that shared a large lot with a sprawling cedar-shingled starter mansion. The cottage had its own gravel driveway that ended next to the front steps. The driveway was empty. I parked, crunched across the gravel, and knocked on the door. No answer. She was probably at work. This was going to take more than a day, so I decided to find a place to stay.

Ten years ago, Fowler and I had attended a police conference at a resort in Hyannis. We drove through town and parked in front of the resort. Fowler, born, raised, and still living in Boston, had climbed out of the car, stretched his massive shoulders, looked around at all the two-story structures, and asked, "Who cut down all the buildings?"

I smiled at the memory as I checked into the same resort, though it was a strange term for a place that looked like a couple of motels tacked onto a conference center. I bought toiletries in the lobby newsstand and decided to grab a quick meal in the restaurant before returning to McKinnon's cottage.

I had almost finished eating when a familiar face appeared at the end of the bar. Joey Manzi—one of Fallon's goons. With long, slicked-back hair, out-of-date sideburns, and a receding chin, he looked like a rock-and-roll rat. Fowler and I had popped him seven years ago for the murder of a Korean shop owner. We had Manzi on ice until our only witness went missing before the trial, and we were forced to cut Manzi loose. Art had to physically restrain me from putting my hands on the punk. What the hell was he doing in Hyannis? He wasn't the curly-headed man, but it couldn't be a coincidence that he was here. I paid the bill and strolled over to get reacquainted.

Manzi was nursing a drink when I sat down next to him and said, "How's it going, Joey?"

"You're earl—" He stopped when he realized I wasn't the person he was meeting. He blinked at me for a couple of seconds until he placed my face. Then his eyes bugged.

I smiled at him and said, "I'm early? I didn't know you were expecting me."

Manzi looked past me as if he were expecting Fowler to be lurking nearby. When he saw that I was alone, he turned back to the TV news, as if ignoring me would make me disappear.

Finally, he spoke. "Whaddya want?"

"I thought you looked unhappy sitting here all alone. So I came over to cheer you up."

Still not looking at me, Manzi muttered, "I don't need you to cheer me up."

"Then how about I cheer you down instead?"

"Look, cop, I ain't doin' nothin' but watching the news."

So Manzi thought I was still a cop—good. "Watching the news can be pretty traumatic, Joseph."

I remembered that Manzi hated to be called Joseph. Something about the nuns when he was a kid. I watched his jaw muscle jump.

"I'm on vacation," he said. "That's legal, far as I know."

I laughed out loud. "Vacation? On Cape Cod? Don't kid a kidder, Jo-Jo. Your idea of a vacation is a couple of grams of coke, a whore, and a card game in Dorchester."

This time he looked at me. His small eyes were murderous. "Don't call me Jo-Jo," he snapped. "I ain't no spook."

"Why, that's a racial slur, Jo-Jo."

Manzi turned back to the television, his eyes blinking. I recalled that he blinked a lot whenever he got rattled. When we nailed him for that murder, he had been batting those lashes like a chorus girl.

I leaned closer, draping my arm over the back of his stool. "Tell you what, Jo-Jo," I said. "You tell me why you're really here, or I'll call a guy I know on the Barnstable P.D. and let him get to know you—see if there are any outstanding warrants—stuff like that."

Manzi's head snapped around. His small brown eyes looked black. "There's no paper out there on me, cop, and I don't have to talk to you about nothing. You got no right to hassle me."

At that moment the phone at the other end of the U-shaped bar rang. The bartender picked it up, listened, then looked around until his eyes reached Manzi. He said something into the receiver, put the phone down and walked to where we sat. A smirk pulled at the corner of his mouth. "Mr. Manzi?" he asked. "There's a call for you." He gestured toward the phone.

Manzi glanced at me, slid out of his seat, and hurried down the bar. He spoke, then listened, glancing back at me. I waved. He swiveled and gave me his back to look at. Still, it wasn't hard to tell that he was having a heated exchange. After a few minutes he hung up and affected a swagger as returned to his seat. He picked up his cigarettes and drained his drink, giving me lots of eye contact now. He licked his lips, put the drink down with a thud, and said, "Leave me the fuck alone."

He stepped back and turned to walk away.

The rage that I had stuffed down during my discussion with Atkinson boiled up again. I grabbed his arm. My fingers found a familiar nerve in his forearm and dug in. The shot of pain put him up on his toes and filled his eyes with a cloud of anger and fear.

"I'll be seeing you and your curly-haired friend soon," I whispered.

He flapped his eyelids some more before he managed to speak. "Leggo," he said.

I released him and he hopped back, rubbing his arm. He opened his mouth but said nothing—perhaps because of what he saw in my eyes. Instead, he spun and scurried away.

I slid off my chair and walked to the service area where the bartender stood. He had witnessed our little exchange. I placed a ten-dollar bill on the bar and gestured toward Manzi, who had stopped to buy cigarettes from a vending machine by the door. "Who called him?"

The bartender, a skinny kid in his mid-twenties, eyed the bill, then shrugged and said, "Some guy, said he wanted to speak to a guy named Manzi, like I'm supposed to know everyone who drinks here. I said I didn't know any Manzis, so this guy says, 'He's a guy who looks like a long-haired rat.'"

The bartender showed some uneven teeth, and his hand slid over the ten. He leaned toward me and said softly, "He does kinda look like a rat, doesn't he?"

"That's because he is one," I said, and followed Manzi into the lobby.

CHAPTER 13

I watched the taillights of Manzi's T-bird slide out of the parking lot and disappear past a neighboring office building. I jotted the plate number down, then looked again at my Porsche. It sat slightly tipped from two flat tires, front and rear, on the driver's side. I squatted to inspect the front tire and found a knife cut just below the rim.

I had followed Manzi through the lobby and into the parking lot. He had paused by his car, thrown me a grin, and climbed in. Whoever phoned him in the bar must have been in the building and preceded Manzi to the parking lot to disable my car. That meant the guy knew what I looked like and what I drove. It had to be Curly. He had seen me with Robbie Atkinson and recognized my car—hardly difficult given the paucity of Porsches on the road around here. I cursed myself for driving something flashy to impress Diane.

Standing there in the fading light, I knew they were both down here looking for Ryerson. If they knew enough about him to come to the Cape, I had to assume they also knew about Jean McKinnon. The Porsche tires would have to wait. I yanked out my cell phone and called a cab.

It was 6:15 when the cab pulled to a stop at the end of Jean McKinnon's gravel driveway. There was still no car parked there. I told the driver to wait and walked up to the small cement porch wrapped in wrought-iron railings. I pressed the doorbell and listened to it ring through the wooden door, which featured a brass-rimmed porthole. The cab engine throbbed in the street, breaking the quiet of the neighborhood.

A nasty thought was already hovering: Curly could have been here already. I used my knuckles on the door with the same result. I fished a penlight out of my jacket and was about to shine it in the circular door window when a car turned into the drive. I stepped back, dropped the light into my pocket and stepped from the porch.

A vintage Toyota Celica, silver and as sleek as a seal, rolled toward me and stopped five feet away. The driver's window slid open far enough to show a woman's green eyes bordered by dark, wavy hair. I could hear jazz playing on the radio. Her eyes left me and the music stopped. She looked back at me and said, "May I help you?"

"Are you Jean McKinnon? It's important that I speak to you."

She lowered the window another six inches. Complementing her striking eyes, she had a straight nose except for what looked like a break halfway down on the left side, and a well-formed mouth, now thin with suspicion. "I've had a long day, and I'm not in the mood for a sales pitch or a religious message."

"I'm here about Jimmy Ryerson."

Her eyes changed. "I'd like you to leave now," she said.

I realized that I was scaring the crap out of her. "I'm Nick Magill. I'm sorry to show up at your house unannounced, but this is very important. My ex-wife was tortured and murdered last night because she was Jimmy Ryerson's therapist. I just drove down from Boston."

She stared at me. "I—I'm sorry to hear that."

"Did Jimmy Ryerson ever mention Diane Zeolla?" I asked.

If she recognized Diane's name, I'd know that McKinnon had seen or spoken to Jimmy Ryerson recently.

She was silent. Her eyes grew distant, and I couldn't read their meaning.

"Look," I said, holding my hands up. "I realize that you don't know me and don't have any reason to trust me, but Jimmy Ryerson is in mortal danger. I'm trying to get him into protective custody, or at least warn him."

Her eyes flashed fear. "Are you a cop or something?"

"Or something. Retired Boston homicide detective. My ex-wife called out of the blue last night, begging me to protect her from a prowler. We hadn't been in touch for years. She told me she thought she'd drawn attention from some bad people because of her association with Ryerson. I drove to her house and found her . . . found her dead. Someone had hurt her badly before she was killed."

I stopped, reading shock and fear on her face. My throat had closed when I said again, out loud, that Diane was dead. I felt tears flooding my eyes. To stop the tears, I cleared my throat and pushed on.

"I think she was killed by the man, or men, who are looking for Jimmy. If they find him, they will kill him too. Because you know him, you may also be in danger. I know this is overwhelming—I don't even know if Diane's death has made the news."

"Wait, how do you know that I know Jimmy Ryerson?"

I hesitated. "Jimmy's friend Robbie Atkinson told me that Jimmy mentioned you. Sounded like he has a crush on you."

Jean McKinnon blinked and said, "I—I've been working a double at the hospital. I haven't heard any news yet." She gathered herself, then said in a clearer voice, "Where was she killed?"

"In her home, in Waltham."

She turned off the car engine, opened the door, and stepped out. She was about five-five and slender. White slacks showed under a tweed car-coat. She then did something that took me off-guard—she touched my arm. "I'm so sorry."

I nodded, her authentic sympathy rendering me unable to speak. I held my tears back in an extreme act of will.

"Look," she said softly. "Can you show me some identification? If you are who you say you are, the least I can do is offer you a cup of coffee."

I took out my wallet, extracted my license, and handed it to her. Her eyes darted from the card to my face and back again before she handed it back. "All right, Nick Magill of Rimfield," she said. "Let me make you a cup of coffee."

"If you don't mind, I'll get rid of the cab and call another one later."

She nodded and turned toward her door. "I'll put the coffee on."

I paid the driver and followed her inside.

CHAPTER 14

I HAD TOLD JEAN McKINNON about driving to Diane's home and finding her body. I told her I believed there were now two men on the Cape looking for Jimmy Ryerson. Her face blanched a little as she sat on a couch facing me.

"That must have been horrible," she said. "I've seen dead people, had them die while I worked to save them, but that was in a hospital. They were people I barely knew."

I didn't want to talk, or even think, about how it made me feel. That only fed the rage and kept me from thinking clearly. "May I call you Jean?" I asked, interrupting her.

"Kin," she said. "Everyone calls me Kin."

"Okay, Kin. What about Jimmy? Have you seen him?"

She nodded. "Off and on. He's down here, but he's drinking. He's come around meetings, even called me once, but he was always half in the wrapper."

"You mean A.A. meetings?"

"Yes," she said, standing up. "Sorry. When you're in recovery and working in the treatment field, you kind of forget that not everyone knows the language. How do you like your coffee, Nick?"

"Black, no sugar," I said.

Kin went into the kitchen and returned with two cups of coffee. "So he's drinking but he sometimes goes to A.A. meetings?"

Kin watched me from the couch. "He's confused and scared. He always drank when he felt that way, so it's hard for him to stop now."

"Do you have any idea where he's staying?"

She shook her head. "I'm not sure. He was at a drinking buddy's the last time I talked to him."

I returned to my chair and sat down. "When was that?"

"Three or four days ago."

"Who's the friend and where does he live?"

"I can't think of his name—wait, Mookie something."

"Mookie?"

"That's it," she said with a smile "It's obviously a nickname, but I don't know his real one. Everyone just calls him Mookie. He lives near Bearse's Way, here in Hyannis."

I set my cup on the small table by my chair. "Do you have an address? Then I'll get out of your hair."

She shook her head. "I don't know exactly where he lives. It's not right on Bearse's Way. He's behind some buildings, hidden away in some scrub pines." She thought for a minute. "I could go with you. I think I can find the dirt drive, but I can't promise. I dropped Jimmy off there once."

"Thanks, but that wouldn't be smart. Not with those two clowns out there. You'd be safer getting out of here and staying with a friend.'"

She glared at me. "These jerks aren't going to drive me out of my own home."

First the Atkinson kid, and now her. The world of the innocent brave. "Look," I said, leaning forward, "These two guys are professional killers. They take lives for money. The one I don't know obviously likes his work. He's the one who killed Diane. The other one, Joey Manzi, isn't much better. We almost put him away a few years ago."

"But?"

"One of his scumbag friends—maybe Curly—got to the witness."

"Back when you were a cop in Boston?"

"Yeah. Manzi thinks I'm still on the force—that may slow him down."

Her eyes widened. "You've talked to him?'"

"That's why I came in a cab." I told her about seeing Manzi at the resort and my slashed tires.

"Why didn't you have him arrested?"

"For what?" I smiled. "Being an asshole?"

Kin pushed her hair back and looked at me intently. "Working in hospitals, I've met a lot of police officers," she said. "You don't seem like one—maybe because you haven't done it for a while."

"Yeah," I said. Or maybe I'm just getting soft, I thought.

The coffee was having its way with me. I asked to use Kin's bathroom and was directed through her bedroom. On the way back to the living room, I paused to look at the bedroom, which was neat, with a double bed and two bureaus. A poster of a photograph by Eliot Porter hung on the wall over the bed. Facing it, over a low dresser, was a row of five black-and-white photographs, all framed in black, with white mats. They were dark, moody shots of Cape Cod landscapes, each featuring some dramatic play of light. Four of the scenes were deserted. The fifth shot featured a barely visible figure walking away down a fog-shrouded beach. Like a pin in a map, the figure anchored the image, but also gave it a chilling sense of loneliness.

I came back to the living room and asked, "Did you take those black-and-whites in there?"

For an instant she looked embarrassed. "Oh, it's just something I like to do for fun." She stood and moved to the tiny kitchen and rinsed out her cup.

"Fun? They're such—" I glimpsed movement at the porthole in the front door. Without thought, my Sig was in my hand. Kin had started walking into the living room, and I pushed her against the wall. Outside, I heard the crunch of footsteps on gravel, running. I killed the lights and eased the door open. No one shot at me, so I went out, keeping low. Tires squealed and a car shot away from the edge of the street where the cab had parked. For the second time that night, I saw the taillights of Joey Manzi's T-bird rocket out of sight. I couldn't see how many people were in the car. They knew who and where Jean McKinnon was.

As I turned back to the cottage, Kin was standing in the doorway. She rubbed her left shoulder as I entered the apartment. "Well," she said. "Forget what I said about you not seeming like a cop."

"Sorry," I said.

"That wasn't a complaint."

CHAPTER 15

I WAS TIRED, MY BACK ACHED. For the second time in less than twenty-four hours I was arguing with someone about personal safety.

"It's not safe for you to stay here," I repeated.

Kin stood in the middle of her living room, her arms folded, her mouth set. She had just repeated her earlier pledge that these creeps, as she called them, were not going to run her off. She was much tougher than she appeared at first. Maybe her good looks made it harder for me to see the steel in her. I had known policewomen who were knockouts and could clean your clock. The difference was, they wore their toughness like armor, right up there in your face. This woman was different. Her toughness was internal. I could see it now in the hardness of her eyes and the set of her shoulders. I wasn't going to be able to frighten her like I had Robbie, so I'd have to try another tack.

"Okay, okay." I held up my hands in surrender. "I'll concede that you're tougher than these guys. Hell, you're probably tougher than anybody. But I worry. My doctor says it's my biggest health problem. He says it makes my blood pressure go up and that makes me susceptible to a stroke."

I saw her face soften, with a hint of a smile.

I continued, "So, for my well-being—certainly not yours—how about you call a friend or a cousin or something, go visit them for a day or two."

She was shaking her head before I finished.

"No?" I asked.

"Both of my girlfriends are working tonight. I don't have any family around here."

"Boyfriend?"

"Nope."

"Okay," I said, "Option two. You check into your own room at the local resort. On me."

She smiled a great smile. Then she shook her head.

"Look," I said. "I need to see Mookie tonight in case Jimmy's there. If they know about you, they may know about Mookie. And, I repeat, they know about you. So, here's a counter-counter offer," I continued. "We get in your car, you show me where Mookie lives, except you drop me off and go for a ride. Come back in an hour. If I'm there, we'll argue some more. If I'm not, you go directly to the police. How's that?"

She frowned and thought for a minute before saying, "I hate just driving around."

"Drive around, please. Stay in well-lighted places. One hour won't kill you."

She winced. "That's a terrible way of putting it."

Before I could answer, she added, "Tell you what, we'll fine tune this while I drive."

It took her three trips around the block before she spotted the dirt lane in an overgrown parcel across from another of the proliferating strip malls on the Cape. The track angled into a copse of pine trees next to a boxy, two-story apartment house. We parked in the lot of the strip mall.

"That's the dirt road. There's an old, rundown cottage just beyond those pines. I gave Jimmy a ride here after a meeting." Her voice softened. "I told him not to stay here. Mookie's always got booze and drugs, and Jimmy was only two days sober."

"Okay, you drive around or visit a friend. And whether you're in the vehicle or not, keep your car doors locked."

Her face looked tired as she nodded.

"Give me an hour," I continued. "I hope it won't take any longer, but if I'm not here, don't wait or investigate. Go to the police."

"Nick, I've been thinking—why not go to the police now?"

"Cops need to have a more solid complaint and a little more to go on. They have too much to do to chase possibilities."

"Whoever looked into my door was not a possibility."

"Right, and I recognized Manzi's vehicle pulling away. But from a cop's perspective, there is more than one old Thunderbird on Cape Cod. The Cape is practically New England's vintage-vehicle capital. Nice Celica, by the way."

She smiled.

"Anyway, we can't point them to where Manzi's vehicle is now. It would be a goose chase. But if you come back here and I'm not standing in plain sight, then you have a place, a person, and a story to take to the cops."

"All right," she said. "I'll be careful."

We swapped phone numbers before I opened the door and stepped out.

"Nick?"

"Yes?" I leaned down to her window.

"You be careful, too. Mookie can be a nasty guy, especially when he drinks."

CHAPTER 16

I CROSSED THE STREET and moved along the overgrown bushes that marked the edge of the dirt track. Fifty or so feet to my right, I could see a few lights still on in the apartment building. As I moved out of sight of the main road, I heard Kin's car drive away.

As I passed a stand of junipers, I could make out the silhouette of the old cottage thirty feet ahead. A dented Mazda pick-up was nosed in close to the porch, like a pig with its snout in a trough. Another car was backed into a clump of scrub pine. Next to it, brambles were devouring the skeleton of another pick-up. No lights were on in the building. I heard no sound except the wind in the pines and the distant hum of late-night traffic.

I crept to the rear of the dented pick-up, and keeping the vehicle between myself and the cottage, I checked the front seat, saw no one, and moved silently to the tilting front steps. I drew my gun and slipped onto the porch. The floorboards groaned under my weight like an injured man. I froze, recalling the sound on the staircase that had warned Robbie Atkinson of Curly's approach. I pressed my back against the wall to the left of the door. I could hear no sound from within. Staying against the wall, I rapped on the door with my left hand. Again, I heard nothing—no stirring, snoring, or mumbling. An icy lump formed in my stomach.

I reached across and tried the doorknob. It turned in my hand. I pushed the door open, pulling back out of the line of fire. The door swung open and banged against the inside wall. As I quick-peeked around the door frame, I smelled it again, riding over the stale smell of the interior—the same fetid odor that had floated up from Diane's basement.

I was too late. Again.

I stepped into the room, low and fast, stopping against the wall to the right of the door. There was no sound, no breathing, no subtle shuffle of a foot bracing for the attack. An upholstered chair pressed against my right shoulder. I used it for cover as I pawed the wall and found a light switch. A dim lamp went on to my left. I scanned the room. It was unoccupied except for a few mismatched pieces of furniture draped with discarded clothes, a splay of engine parts and empty beer cans on the floor, and, in the middle of it all, a fat, very dead man.

The wallet in the dead man's jeans identified him as Malcolm Davis, presumably Mookie. He lay curled in a fetal position. He had a small-caliber wound in the left temple, two broken fingers, and fresh cigarette burns on one arm. His dead eyes stared out of a bloated face, and his belly lay in an inert mass on the floor.

I was certain this was the work of the curly-headed man. From what I knew of Manzi, this was not his style. Curly was a psycho and a sadist, but he was also a pro, and so far, he was one step ahead of me and his victims.

I methodically searched the cottage, trying not to disturb anything and equally careful not to leave any of my own fingerprints. On the floor next to Mookie's bed lay a torn matchbook cover with a hand-scribbled phone number. I squatted down but didn't pick it up. No name, just the number. It could ring Davis's drug dealer, his bookie, or a man or woman with a taste for gone-to-seed addicts. The matchbook was not dog-eared or worn, so maybe its newness meant something. Maybe it would lead to Jimmy Ryerson. I pulled my cell from my back pocket and entered the number under "Matchbook." At this point, I was willing to grasp at straws.

My phone clock told me I'd been in this squalid dump for about forty-five minutes. I used my handkerchief to turn off the light after I had wiped the switch and let myself out, wiping for prints as I went. The air smelled sweet after the stench of the cottage. I had already decided to notify the police anonymously again. I knew it would be a long day of questioning if they caught me, maybe even a night in jail while they cleared me as a suspect. I couldn't afford to get tied up while Ryerson was out there with Curly and Manzi on the hunt.

When I reached the end of the dirt track, I saw Kin's car parked in the mall lot. I hurried across the street and climbed in.

"You're early," I said as she handed me a cup of coffee. "And you stopped for coffee."

She shrugged. "Guess I'm not too trainable. Besides, I thought you might need rescuing."

"Mookie was the one who needed rescuing, but I was too late. Listen, we need to get out of here."

Her face froze. "You mean—?"

"He's dead. The signature says he got killed by the same guy who murdered Diane."

"Oh my God," she said, staring at me. "Shouldn't we call the police or something?"

I nodded. "In a minute, but let's get out of here before anyone sees us. Your car is memorable. Pull over in a couple of blocks."

Kin pulled the car around and onto the street.

CHAPTER 17

WE STOPPED ON MAIN STREET, and I called in the murder. Mookie's death had demolished Kin's sense of invincibility, and she agreed that going home was out of the question. She drove to the resort and parked across the lot from my disabled Porsche.

"There's another number I need to call," I said, telling her about the matchbook. She nodded as I pressed the call button and held the phone to my ear. The line rang eight or nine times before I hung up. "Nada," I said.

"Well, it is the middle of the night for most people."

"Speaking of which," I said. "I need a couple of hours' sleep. You do, too. I strongly suggest you don't go in to work tomorrow."

"I have the next four days off. That's why I worked the double. I wanted some time off to relax." She gave me a twisted smile. "This wasn't what I had in mind."

"I certainly hope not."

"What now?"

"We go into the lobby. I'll go first, check for Manzi or the cretin with curly hair. If it looks clear, I'll come back to my car and give you a wave. Register under an assumed name. I have enough money for you to pay cash. So pick a name and we'll do it."

Kin nodded. My cell rang—Art Fowler.

"Got a name for you," he said. "Dwayne Hanson. Sound familiar?"

"No. Who is he?"

"Hired hitter. A real sicko. Fallon uses him for collections and enforcement, mostly. The psycho fuck's been real lucky so far. Only done time once, in juvie, for robbery and assault. Since then he's been a suspect in at least five homicides, and the OC task force thinks those are just the tip of the iceberg."

"Sounds like my guy. And he just left another body in his wake. I phoned it in to the Barnstable P.D. about fifteen minutes ago. Anonymously."

"Who's the vic, the Ryerson kid?"

"No, a guy named Malcolm 'Mookie' Davis. Some poor slob Ryerson was rumored to be staying with. Just a drunk civilian, not in the life, as far as I know."

"Shit," Fowler muttered. "Watch yourself, Nick. I found out that eighteen years ago Hanson was picked up as a suspect in the murder of his father."

"No shit."

"Yep. The father was a leg breaker for Vincent Fallon, Frankie's old man. Brutal bastard. He had a sheet as long as your arm, including domestics. He apparently beat the shit out of his wife, kids, and girlfriends on a regular basis. Of course, no one ever filed charges."

"What makes you think Hanson took out the old man?"

"Timing," Art said. "Young Dwayne had just wrapped up that robbery-assault bit. He was sprung on a Thursday and the old man got his reward on Saturday."

"How?"

"Shot to death in a vacant lot. Looked like there was a hell of a fight first. The gun was never found, and they had no witnesses, so the seventeen-year-old Hanson walked. They always say that juvie is grad school for criminals."

"Jesus. Did he marry his mother?"

Fowler chuckled. "She died of cancer six months later."

"So much for happy endings," I said, watching Kin trying to track our exchange.

"Yeah," Art said. "By the way, the T-bird's registered to some guy named Ike Knowlton. He runs a junk yard in Falmouth. It hasn't been reported, so I don't know what the deal is."

"Thanks, Art."

"Wait a minute, buddy. The Feebs called me. They're looking for you."

"What the hell for?"

"They displayed their usual warmth and openness, so I have no idea."

"What did you tell them?"

"Said I hadn't heard from you in months. I wouldn't tell the Feebs anything unless they dropped trou' and showed me what they had first."

I snorted. "Thanks, Art, I'll never un-see that. Hey, can I get one more favor? Can you check a number in the reverse directory? I need an address."

"Oh, hell, I'm in this far—is it a land line? Otherwise we can't do jack."

"No idea," I said.

"Give me the number."

I read it to him off the matchbook cover. He verified it and gave me an address. "Thanks, partner," I said. "I'll stay in touch."

"Watch yourself, Nick."

After I made sure the lobby was clear, I signaled Kin, and she registered. As agreed, she flashed her fingers to let me know her room number—243. I waited until she was out of sight before crossing the lobby on the way to my room.

"Excuse me, Mr. Magill." It was the desk clerk who had registered me.

I went to the counter.

"There were two gentlemen here looking for you earlier this evening," he said. "One of them left a business card." He held it out to me as if it were radioactive.

The card identified Agent Harold Carter of the Federal Bureau of Investigation. A phone number was penned in at the bottom. So the Feebs had found me.

"He asked that you call him whenever you returned. No matter how late it was. They're staying at the Days End Inn," he sniffed. "Next to the mall."

"Thanks," I said. Somehow, my whereabouts were being monitored by the feds. *How was that possible? And what the hell did they want?*

Art was the only one I'd talked to since leaving Boston, and he wouldn't give them a cold drink in hell. I didn't tell Robbie Atkinson where I was. That left Dwayne Hanson and Manzi. I couldn't picture either one of them snuggling up with the very people who wanted to put them away.

My thoughts were tumbling all over themselves as I went to my room and called Kin.

"Do you have two beds?" I asked.

"Yes, two doubles. Why?"

"I need to use one. There are some other people who know I'm here. Not the two I'm looking for, but I don't want to see them. I'll explain when I get there."

"Ah, Nick—I . . ."

"Don't worry," I said. "Romance is the absolute last thing on my mind tonight."

CHAPTER 18

KIN AND I MADE FOR AWKWARD ROOMMATES at first, but after I explained the unexpected arrival of the feds and she trusted that my motives were pure, we settled in. I also filled her in on my chat with Art Fowler. Then we crashed. Kin took the bed closest to the slider, and I lay on the one by the door. Except for her sweater and shoes, she slid into bed fully clothed. I stretched out on top of the bedspread, my hand resting on the butt of my holstered gun. I dropped into sleep almost immediately.

I awoke with a start when I heard Kin calling my name. I sat up, blinking, my gun half drawn.

"Whoa," she squawked. "It's me. I brought us some coffee."

I swung my legs over the side of the bed and pawed at my face. "You went out for coffee?"

"Just downstairs, to the hotel restaurant. I have muffins, too."

I checked my watch. It was 6:50 a.m. I stood and stretched. "I didn't even hear you leave. I don't usually sleep that soundly."

"You probably don't usually go for two days without sleep."

I nodded and took the coffee she held out to me. It was damned near battery acid, but it had caffeine in it.

"What are your plans?" she asked, perching on the edge of her bed, opposite me.

"I've got to get my tires fixed. There's a gas station across the street."

"I'll take a shower while you're doing that."

"Sure. But first, let's try calling the number on the matchbook again."

I punched the number and it started to ring. I put the phone on speaker and laid it on the bedspread next to me. She moved over to sit next to me and studied the phone. Again, it rang without an answer. When I ended the call, Kin looked at me with a quizzical expression.

"This number seems familiar, but I can't place it," she said.

"Art gave me an address from the reverse directory. It's someplace in Provincetown."

Her face lit up. "Why didn't you say so? I'm almost positive it's a halfway house."

"Hm," I said. "Then why the hell doesn't somebody answer the phone?"

"Could be an old landline that nobody uses, because it only gets spam calls. That's what I use my land line for," she said. "So you have a street address?"

I told her the address. It didn't ring a bell, but she said she'd never actually been to the place. We agreed that driving to Provincetown was today's mission.

I took a quick shower and walked over to the gas station while Kin used the shower. There were two new tires on the Porsche by 9:15. I parked by the hotel and walked into the lobby. Two gray-suited men stood at the reception desk. I made them for feds even before I overheard them talking to the clerk. The taller of the two, a stocky man with short blond hair, said, "Your night man told us he checked in yesterday afternoon."

The day clerk didn't know me. He punched keys on his computer, then nodded. "Yessir, he's in room 128. And he hasn't checked out yet."

The blond man looked at his partner, who was three inches shorter with a black brush cut. Brush cut nodded.

"Excellent," said the blond guy. "Thank you," he said. They turned and walked in the direction of my room. The clerk watched them go.

I crossed to the counter and leaned on it. "Checkout for Melanie Berger—room 243." This was Kin's alias. The clerk punched buttons again, and a bill cranked out of the printer. "Boy, those guys look tough," I said. "If I didn't know better, I'd think they were cops."

He tore it off and handed it to me. "You're close," he said, *sotto voce*. "They're FBI agents."

I knocked on 243—twice, then once, as we had agreed. Kin opened the door, her face alive with excitement. "I've been calling that number, and someone finally answered. I think Jimmy is staying there, but he isn't in the building now," she said.

"Good, let's go. The feds are in my hotel room. It might take them a while to figure out I'm not there, and by then we should be clear of this place."

"Is that a cop joke?"

"Yeah, a pretty lame one. Let's go."

I had planned to register Kin under a different false name, change rooms, and ask her to stay put for the day. But she convinced me that the Ryerson boy trusted her, and she knew how to navigate the recovery house terrain. I reluctantly agreed to take her with me. We left by a side door and circled the hotel. There was no sign of the two scumbags or my federal friends.

We drove in separate cars to a supermarket, left the Celica in the parking lot, and she climbed into the Porsche. The Celica had been ID'd by Manzi. "Can you give me directions to Provincetown, or should I use the app?"

She gave me a smile that I felt in my solar plexus. "We should be there in less than an hour," Kin said. "Do you know how to get to Route 6?"

CHAPTER 19

W<small>E GRABBED SOME BETTER COFFEE</small> at a local espresso place before hitting the highway.

"So the place in Provincetown. Is it basically a crash pad?"

She gave me a sharp look. "More like a safe house for alcoholics and addicts who are trying to stay sober after they detox in a hospital or treatment facility. They can hole up there until life starts to make sense."

"Let me know when that happens." I meant it to be funny, but it came out marinated in sarcasm.

Kin was quiet for a few moments. "Nick, do you drink?" Her tone was delicate.

"What? No, as a matter of fact I don't. My father was a stone drunk who died homeless. My brother's on the same path, if he isn't already there. You may have noticed that I don't have a lot of patience with alcoholics—active ones, anyway."

Kin said, "I'm an alcoholic, you know, and not a high-bottom one, either. My story isn't pretty. Carrying that feels worse for women sometimes, because of the added level of shame. Women are mothers, and mothers are saints. Even if you're not a mother, you're held to the same standard if you're female."

"Huh," I said. My throat felt dry. This territory was a minefield for me. I never said the right thing, so my usual M.O. was to jump around blowing up the mines to get rid of the tension and see where all the pieces landed. This time I just swallowed and changed the subject.

"Is the halfway house we're going to a secret? I don't imagine many people want one in their neighborhood."

"It's sort of a secret, since they don't advertise it, and it doesn't follow the usual treatment guidelines," Kin said. "A nurse swings by periodically, but her services are not covered by insurance. I guess I'd describe it as an informal place." She thought for a moment. "Well, it's got so many rules I guess it's not really that informal. More like minimalist, bare bones."

"Who runs it?"

"A handful of people who got sober there. A couple of guys started it fifteen or twenty years ago. One of them is dead now. The other's semi-retired. He's been sober since the Stone Age."

We rounded the Orleans rotary. The landscape opened to reveal a pond.

"If they don't take insurance, how do they support themselves?"

"I'm not sure. People pay whatever they can toward the overhead, do some chores. Folks who got sober there send contributions." She looked at me. "Speaking of which, how do you support yourself, now that you're not a cop anymore?"

"If you don't mind my asking," I said.

Her laugh had a nice sound. "You don't mind, do you?"

I shrugged. "I do whatever I want, I guess. Right now I've been doing some sculpting."

"You're a sculptor?"

I smiled. "No, I sculpt. There's a difference."

"Are you telling me you're one of those independently wealthy types?"

"Are you always this subtle when you question people?"

She raised her eyebrows. "Maybe I should've been a cop, huh?"

I shrugged. "You're certainly blunt enough to be one."

Her smile faded, but only a little. "Have I offended you?"

I looked at her and laughed. "No. It's just that I'm not used to people asking me direct questions about my source of income. They usually sneak up on it in conversation and try not to appear rude or inquisitive, but manage to be both."

"Well, at least I'm not like most people."

"Certainly not," I said.

"So?" She wasn't letting me off the hook.

"So, I got my money the old-fashioned American way."

"You earned it?"

"I inherited it."

She laughed. "Your father was wealthy?"

"Definitely not my father," I said. "It came from my mother's brother, Uncle Frank."

"Were you close to him?"

"Not particularly, though he got my father out of our house, and I was pretty damned grateful for that. But every summer, he'd take his son, Bud, and me to a working farm he had in Maine."

"He had a son and he wasn't close to you—why did he leave you money?"

I glanced at her again. "You should've been a cop."

"If you don't want to talk about it . . ."

"It's okay. When I was seventeen and Bud was around fourteen or fifteen, we spent a day working in the field, from first light to late afternoon. It was that kind of humid-hot day that makes you feel as if your bones have melted. We decided to reward ourselves with a swim as soon as we finished.

"The ocean up there is really cold. We had a good swim, but Bud insisted on going back in before we left. He cramped up, so I went in and got him. No big deal. I just towed him in until I could touch bottom and then carried him in the shallows. He had taken in some water, but he was okay, just scared. I got him squared away and took him home. I never mentioned it to Uncle Frank. In fact, I forgot about it until five years ago."

"What happened?"

"Frank died and left me a big chunk of money. Apparently Bud had told him. Uncle Frank never mentioned it to me, but obviously he didn't forget."

"How did he earn his money—or was that inherited too?"

"I guess he was some sort of genius in business. He would have made a great poker player. Never said much, never showed much, so you never knew what he was thinking. Except for that time when he arrived to watch my father pack. There was no mistaking his meaning that day."

Kin was quiet, and I could see she was holding back more questions about that one. "Your turn," I said. "Tell me about you."

"I'm a registered nurse. I'm eight years clean and sober, and I grew up in California."

"Where in California?"

"San Diego. Actually, Coronado, an island right by the city."

"Yeah, I've been there, stayed at the Hotel Del Coronado."

"Yes, the Del is a famous place. We lived at the other end of the island, near the naval base. My father was in the Navy."

"A career guy?"

"Yes." She stared out the windshield, silent, lost in thought. Then she turned in the seat, as if physically pulling herself back from her past. "My father was a Navy Seal. He trained the guys who tried to become Seals."

I had run into Seals when I was an MP. "Tough guys," I said. "It takes a lot to become one."

Her chuckle had a bitter edge. "Probably not more than it takes to live with one."

"A hard guy."

"Real hard when he drank. He was always strict, but as time went on . . ." She fell silent again.

Was everybody's old man a drunk? "It's hard, isn't it?" I said, almost to myself.

Kin pulled her eyes away from the highway. "Yes," she said, "I tried to measure up until high school, then I started to rebel." She tapped her index fingers together. "We were constantly butting heads. My brother and sister were grown and long gone. So I guess he got it in his head that I was his last chance at making a perfect kid."

"He didn't succeed?"

"Not even close. I barely finished high school. Managed to get into the state college, then promptly partied my way out."

"So you drank, even with your father's drinking?"

"I was going to do it right," she said. "I wouldn't have the same trouble he had."

"It didn't work, eh?"

"Not only did I wind up drinking like he did, I threw pot and coke into the mix. It made for a real mess."

I turned to look at this beautiful woman sitting there talking about her alcoholism and drug abuse. She seemed fairly comfortable talking about it, which I found hard to believe. "But you're a registered nurse."

"That happened in sobriety. When I was using, I'd take a course here, a course there, but I couldn't get anything going."

"But you stopped drinking and all the other stuff," I said, tapping the steering wheel for emphasis. "It took a lot of strength to quit and follow your dream."

"Well, first of all, I had a lot of help in stopping. I didn't do it all by myself. And second, I don't know if nursing is my dream. Some days I like it. Some days I'd rather be waiting tables."

"Is your family still in California?"

"My mom lives in San Diego. My father dropped dead four years ago. My brother, who had moved to Texas, was killed in a car crash a year later. Drunk. My sister is somewhere in the Chicago area."

"You kids certainly scattered."

"That's what happens when everyone is running for their lives." Scrub pines dropped away on the right, revealing a sliver of flat, pewter ocean.

"Do you have any more siblings, other than the alcoholic brother?" Kin asked.

"No. Father, mother, my brother and me."

"Where do you come from originally?"

"South Boston. A legendary breeding ground for criminals and drunks. And cops, of course."

"What did your dad do?"

"He worked for a while at Uncle Frank's electronics company, then at a couple of smaller companies. He was a machinist. Then he couldn't work anymore because of the drinking. He died homeless."

"I'm sorry," she said.

I realized that my arms were extended, my hands on the wheel at ten and two o'clock. My damn knuckles were white.

"Look, my father was a drunk. It's ancient history now."

"Are your mother and father still living?"

"They died years ago."

"And your brother?"

I pried a hand off the steering wheel and gestured dismissively. "I have no idea where he is. He's not part of my life anymore. And if he's still drinking, which he probably is, good riddance."

She was staring at me.

"What?" I asked. I heard the tension in my voice.

"No mother," she said softly. "No father. No brother. And you don't drink. So no problem?"

"That's right. So what?"

"I was just wondering, because it sure sounds like you're choking on somebody's drink."

I didn't respond, because if I opened my mouth, I'd take her head off. We didn't speak for almost ten minutes during which time a light drizzle began to fall. Finally, as we entered Truro, I had cooled off enough to break the silence. "What's the name of this halfway house?"

"It's called Riley's. The men who founded it were Warren and O'Malley. I was told Riley was one of their first recovering guys. He stayed sober but was hit by a car and killed. They named the place after him."

I nodded my head slowly, thinking. I had more questions, but my father kept crowding my thoughts. I pushed the old man away again by saying, "Maybe they should have named it Riley's Last Resort."

"Not bad," she said. "There's a saying: When you get to the end of your rope, tie a knot in it and hang on. People who come to Riley's are clinging to the threads of that knot."

I glanced at her. Our eyes met, and I felt my anger begin to drain. "Let's hope Jimmy Ryerson doesn't let go," I said.

CHAPTER 20

It was almost 10:30 when we drove into Provincetown. The drizzle had turned into a steady rain, smudging the line between sea and sky. Both dominated the view on this long peninsula curling into the sea. I had been here a few times in my life but hadn't visited for years. The natural landscape preserved in the Cape Cod National Seashore was stunning, but the summer crowds in the narrow streets were not for me.

"Turn here," said Kin, and I turned onto Bradford Street. Low clapboard houses lined each side of the street. The wipers moved rhythmically across the Porsche's windshield.

"Spring in Provincetown can be as miserable as summer in San Francisco," Kin said absently.

"Don't worry, it'll be spring by mid-June—just in time for the tourists."

"My favorite seasonal event," she said.

We slowly drove the length of Bradford Street until it ended over an expanse of marsh and dunes. The sea beyond was the color of an old nickel.

Kin shook her head and sighed. "I'm sorry, Nick, I don't remember which turn to take. It's time for your maps program to take over."

She repeated the address to me and I typed it into my phone. Prompted by a robotic female voice, I swung the car around in a condo parking lot and headed back the way we had come. After a few more turns, it was clear that the app was two steps behind in the dense matrix of streets.

"Sometimes you still have to ask people," I said. I stopped in front of a market and climbed out of the car into a raw, wind-driven rain. It felt ten degrees colder than Hyannis.

Inside the store, a heavy-set young man in a soiled white apron stood at the register, thumbing through a copy of *People.* He was absently picking at his chin.

"Excuse me," I said. "I'm looking for a place called Riley's. It's on one of the streets off Bradford."

The young man glanced up from the magazine and shrugged. "Never heard of it," he muttered. His eyes went back to the magazine.

I looked at him. America's future.

"Anyone here who might know? It's important."

The young man's thumb popped out. He gestured over his shoulder toward the back of the store. "Back there." His eyes never left the magazine.

I walked down an aisle to a meat counter. Behind it, an older, female version of the television aficionado was cutting meat, dressed in a white smock. A smaller, gray-haired woman stood by the counter watching her. They both turned to look at me.

"Good morning. Do either of you know where a place called Riley's is located? I believe it's on a street off Bradford."

The older woman shook her head and looked inquiringly at the butcher, who put down her carving knife and wiped her hands on her smock, leaving pink smears. She frowned and asked, "Is it a private home? I've never heard of a restaurant by that name."

"No, it's a halfway house for alcoholics to get sober."

The older woman stepped back and clucked her tongue disapprovingly. "So that's what they call that place. It ought to be shut down. I hear drug addicts go there, too. Disgraceful."

She turned to the butcher. "You know the place, Syl. It's where all the bums go."

Syl, the meat cutter, nodded, retrieved her knife, and pointed with it. "You go back toward the East End. Bradley's on your left. Dodge is your first right. I think it's the last house on the left."

That figures, I thought. I thanked them and left.

"I've got directions," I said, as I slid into the idling Porsche.

"Great," Kin said. "By the way, your cell phone rang while you were in the market."

"Did you answer it?"

"It was Art Fowler. He took the time to warn me—after I introduced myself—that you are—" She paused, tipping her head in thought. "I believe 'a prevert' were his exact words. Of course, I thanked him for the warning."

"What are friends for?" I punched his number into the phone and smiled. "A prevert?" I asked when he answered.

Art chuckled. "Well, you were only a pervert when I met you. Clearly you've mutated, over the years."

"I'm delighted that you chose to share my improvement with Ms. McKinnon."

"You can call her Kin," Art said. "Everybody does."

"Thank you, Mr. Fowler. What have you got for me?"

"Nothing much. I'm just calling to keep tabs on you now that I'm not around to protect you."

"I do appreciate your concern. Speaking of concerns, the feds found out that I was at the resort in Hyannis."

"What? How the hell did they do that?"

"Good question. This all just gets curiouser and curiouser."

"We're not on speakerphone, are we, Nick?"

"No, why?"

"I'm just wondering how smart it is to have this woman along? Hanson's a dangerous guy, and we both know about Manzi."

Art was right, but here I was in Provincetown with her. "I couldn't get rid of her," I said, trying to keep my tone light. "She's one stubborn woman." I watched that big smile creep across her face. "On the plus side," I went on, "she knows Ryerson, and he trusts her."

"She's a civilian, Nick. She sounds like a nice person. Keep her out of harm's way."

"Agreed," I said, making eye contact with her. "You say you think she's a nice person? Well, you're a full-time detective, so I guess I'll have to accept your assessment."

As we looked at each other, her face seemed to open and soften. Art Fowler snapped the mood like a dry twig. "Speaking of harm's way, where are you, wild man?"

"Provincetown. We think Ryerson may be sobering up here."

"We do, huh? Would we like the name of a cop we can talk to on the Provincetown PD?"

Art regularly attended police conferences and conventions. The joke was that Art Fowler may have met a cop he didn't like, but he'd never met one he didn't remember.

"Thanks, that might be helpful."

"Let me give him a call."

I didn't want some local yokel cramping my play. "That's not necessary, Art. I don't need an introduction."

"Hah," he snorted. "At the rate you're going, you may need a lot more than an introduction. I'm making the call."

I knew there was no sense arguing. "Thanks, Mom," I said.

"Wear your mittens," he replied and hung up.

CHAPTER 21

"THAT'S THE HOUSE, up there."

Kin pointed to a dark green building with a wide porch. There were two stories, plus what looked to be a finished attic with curtains covering a window in the eaves. A long wooden staircase, freshly repaired in several places, climbed the hill to the porch.

As she stepped out of the car, Kin turned her collar up against the wind-driven rain. The damp chill cut through my cotton coat. We hurried up the staircase and onto the shelter of the porch. White wooden chairs lined the front porch facing the harbor. From our vantage point, we could see the spire of a church as it pushed above a grove of twisted pines behind a small cape house across the street. Without those windbreaks, it seemed even colder.

A heavy metal doorknocker decorated the center of a windowless black door. It was hinged at the top in a wide V with the bottom in the form of a flying seagull. It appeared to be very old, pitted and stained by years in the salt air. I lifted its surprisingly heavy weight and let it swing against the door.

I was about to drop it for the third time when the door opened wide enough to frame the face and part of the body of a Black man, who peered out at us with a look of irritation. He was over six feet tall and muscular, wearing a deep-green, long-sleeved T-shirt. His bald head was long and narrow. Heavily lidded eyes gave him a sleepy look. His nose had been broken more than once, and a scar began in the middle of his left eyebrow and ended somewhere near the top of his skull. His dark skin seemed to reflect the gray ocean light.

"What can I do for you folks?"

Although his voice was soft, with a slight southern edge, it was not welcoming.

"We're looking for Jimmy Ryerson," I said.

The man shook his head. "Can't help you, pardner."

He started to close the door. I put my hand on it to keep it from shutting. "Look," I said, leaning my weight on it. "I realize you probably have rules here, but this is an emergency. If the boy's here, he's in real danger."

The man's hooded eyes focused on my hand. "Move your damn paw, mister."

I kept my hand where it was. "Two of his friends have been murdered. The killers may be in Provincetown now."

"Get your fuckin' hand off my door."

Kin stepped around me.

"Excuse me, mister . . . ?" she said, attempting a smile.

His sleepy eyes moved to her.

"My name is Jean McKinnon. Jimmy knows me by my nickname, Kin. I'm a nurse at the detox in Hyannis. Jimmy was a patient there a while ago." She paused. "I also see him at meetings."

The man thought for a second, then said to me, "Back off, man. I'll come out and we'll talk."

I dropped my hand and stepped back. The door closed. I touched Kin's shoulder. "Thanks."

The door reopened and the man stepped out, buttoning a navy pea coat. He closed the door and offered his hand, first to Kin, then to me.

"Call me Johnson," he said. "You can't come in. We got a lotta rules here. They can't be fucked with."

"We understand," Kin said. "The hospital has the same rules."

Johnson smiled for the first time. I could see where teeth had been knocked out and replaced by bridgework.

"What they call you?" he asked me.

"Nick Magill."

"Can we get a message to Jimmy?" Kin asked.

"Shit. You know I can't even tell you if he's here. Deliverin' messages ain't something I do."

"We respect that, but if he's here, the whole house is in danger," I said. "The guys who are hunting Jimmy Ryerson will come in here and blow your ass into the next world and not look back. If we found you, they will too."

Johnson turned his collar up and rammed his hands deep into his pockets. He looked at both of us. "I hear you," he said slowly. "But I can't do what you ask. Thanks for the warning. We'll be real careful."

"Unless you're armed," I said, "real careful won't count for shit."

Johnson's eyes got sleepy again. He shook his head.

Kin put her hand on my arm and nodded toward the street. "Let's go," she said. "We'll go with Plan B."

I raised my eyebrows. "Plan B?"

"Plan B, shit," Johnson said, shaking his head. "I gotta go."

We turned toward the stairs as Johnson opened the door to go inside. I stopped and looked back at him.

"Hey, Johnson," I said. "You're a stand-up guy, but in this game, stand-up guys make the best targets."

Johnson nodded and watched us start down the stairs, then went inside and closed the door.

I heard the lock turn.

When we were back in the Porsche, I started the engine and turned the heater up. I looked at Kin. "So, there's a Plan B?"

"No, but we were at a dead end, and I wanted to leave instead of standing there arguing," she said with a sheepish grin. "Now what should we do?"

"Well, now that you've salvaged our credibility with the intractable Mr. Johnson, I'll have to reveal Plan C."

She hugged herself. "Well, do it fast because I'm freezing."

I put the car in gear. "We're buying sweaters," I said. "And then we're going to see a cop."

CHAPTER 22

Mᴀɴɴʏ Bᴀᴛɪꜱᴛᴀ, the Provincetown officer Art Fowler knew, was out on a case. The desk sergeant, a heavy-set man with liquid brown eyes, had no idea when Batista would return. This lack of knowledge didn't seem to trouble him at all. He scratched a bulbous nose, eyed Kin for the tenth time, and made a half-hearted offer to call another officer.

I left Art Fowler's name, since it would have more clout than mine, and promised to return within the hour. That did not excite the sergeant either.

Outside, we ran through the cold, wind-driven rain to the car. We had stopped at a sporting goods store for sweaters and a change of clothes for Kin before coming to the police station, so at least we were warm.

"I know a place that has the best kale soup ever made," Kin said.

I love kale soup. "The best ever?" I asked.

"Absolutely. It's on Commercial Street a block past the town hall, down an alley. The restaurant's right on the water."

"The way it's raining, the place will probably be underwater."

Kin smiled. "The best kale soup in the world is worth holding your breath for."

"This really is great soup," I said, feeling its warmth spread through my belly. My coat dripped onto the floor from the back of an extra chair at our table.

"It's all part of McKinnon's Guide to Cape Cod," Kin said.

"But you can call her Kin—everybody does."

She laughed. "I guess I'd better change my rap."

"If this soup is an example of your guide services, you can do anything you like."

"Thank you, kind sir," she said. She looked out of the rain-streaked window next to us. Her face became more thoughtful. When she turned back to me, she smiled. "Tell me about what you've done with your life since Uncle Frank so radically changed it."

It threw me. Five months after Diane had hooked up with her supervisor, Uncle Frank's inheritance had yanked me out of the rut of needing to do police work. I had thought of calling Diane and pursuing her because I still loved her, but I could never bring myself to make that phone call.

"That wasn't a trick question," Kin said, cracking my introspection. "And you don't have to answer it if you don't want to."

"Sorry," I said. "That's a good question, considering everything that's happened in the past two days."

"If you don't want to . . ."

I touched her hand. "No, it's okay." It was my turn to stare out at the now-choppy ocean. "I left police work and traveled at first—to the Southwest, Europe— sort of bumming around. I was trying to decide what I wanted to do. Finally, I took a drawing class. I had always doodled, so it seemed a logical thing to try." I stirred my soup. "Anyway, my drawings weren't horrible, so I tried painting. That didn't turn out as well as I had hoped. One day I was having coffee with a woman from my painting class and she suggested sculpting."

Kin ran a hand through her wavy hair, then sipped her soup. "Were you always in police work before Uncle Frank?"

I nodded. "First, the military police, then the Boston P.D."

"I guess I'm a little surprised that you didn't go private. Set up your own security company or something like that."

"Too much paperwork. That's what I hated about police work."

"Paperwork—my favorite." She laughed. "There's an endless amount of that at the hospital."

"I can imagine. Anyway, my uncle's business manager took the inheritance and invested it—with impressive results. The guy's got financial radar as far as I'm concerned."

She finished her soup and sipped her coffee. "It sounds as if you've made some exciting choices."

I remembered the cracks by other cops when I told them I was going to art school: "You just wanna check out naked broads," or "What the hell you wanna hang out with a buncha dope-smoking hippies for?" A lot of that stuff, except for Art, who said, "Why not?"

"Where do you do your sculpting?"

"I built a house with a studio in the Berkshires."

"Do you exhibit?"

"No, not really," I said.

"Define 'not really.'"

She was merciless. "Uh . . ." I stammered. "Well, I have a field with some of my sculptures in it . . . outside my home."

She studied my face. "I'd like to see your sculptures sometime."

I finished my soup. Having someone come all that way just to see my work made me feel vulnerable. Not a comfortable feeling.

"It's a long drive out there," I said.

"I'll bet I've driven farther, and for less reason."

Those green eyes were boring into me. I wiped my mouth and tossed enough money on the table to cover the meal and tip.

She smiled. "Are we leaving?"

"Yeah. We better see if Batista is back at the station."

"First, finish what we started to talk about."

"What?"

"Your sculpture—as in my seeing it."

"Oh, yeah. Well, I guess, if you really don't mind driving all that way . . ."

"Great," she said with a grin. "I'll look forward to it."

The wind had intensified, whipping the rain and making it feel a lot colder. We stood in the restaurant's covered doorway with the sea moaning behind us. "This keeps up, we're going to need some rain gear," I said.

We headed into an alley that led out to the street where the Porsche was parked, squeezing past a dumpster.

"I want to pay you back for all these purchases." She stopped, distracted by a van backing into the alley. The image of a large blue fish covered its rear doors.

"Must be a delivery," Kin said. "We ought to get out of the way."

At that moment, the van stopped. Its driver's door opened and Joey Manzi slid out, wearing a savage grin.

"Hey, asshole," he called, pointing at me. "You ain't a cop anymore."

I grabbed Kin. "Run back to the restaurant, quick."

As I stepped toward the advancing Manzi, I heard Kin gasp and call my name. I started to turn when a burst of pain exploded from the back of my head. A blinding white flash flooded my vision before I toppled into a place with no light at all.

CHAPTER 23

LIKE SMELLING SALTS, the stench of dead fish pulled me out of the blackness. I lay on my side. My head throbbed, but when I tried to touch it, I found my arms were bound. I struggled and realized that my ankles were tied as well. Voices came from above my head. We were moving. I worked my eyes open, then had to fight a wave of nausea. I lay on the damp, stinking metal floor of the fish van.

Kin was wedged between the bucket seats with her back against the engine console. A hand gripped her tousled hair. A strip of duct tape covered her mouth.

"My goodness, you're a fine-looking woman."

It was a voice I didn't recognize. When I tried to speak, I found my mouth was taped, too.

I twisted on the floor and peered up at a horse-faced man with curly hair as he leaned over from the passenger seat to sniff Kin's hair. Dwayne Hanson.

"Oooh," he cooed, "you smell yummy." He stroked her cheek.

Kin's eyes danced with anger and fear as she tried to pull her head away.

"How about up there?" I recognized Manzi's voice.

"Sure, Joey. Whatever you think. My new honey and I are getting to know each other."

The van swung to the right and began bouncing over an uneven road. After a minute of straining and rocking, we stopped.

"Good, it's still boarded up for the winter." Manzi again.

They climbed out of the van and left us inside. A raw cold filled the interior, telling me that they had left the front doors open. The chill revived me. My eyes met Kin's. Now she looked scared. I winked at her. What the hell.

We heard glass breaking. A minute or two later, the rear doors opened, letting in a blast of frigid rain. Hands grabbed my ankles and pulled. I was yanked out of the van and smacked my damaged head on the bumper an instant before I hit the ground. My vision sparked, then cleared. Dwayne Hanson leaned over me with a keyboard grin under eyes that were as opaque and dark as the windows in an abandoned house.

"Honey, we're home," Hanson said.

Manzi grabbed me under the arms, Hanson took my feet, and they lugged me into a weatherworn beach shack. Inside, they tossed me onto the floor of the one-room structure and went back outside. I struggled into a sitting position. The room was about thirty by forty feet with a small kitchenette behind a crudely built counter. Bunk beds stood along the left wall. I was on the floor, six or seven feet from an old couch that sat in the middle of the room, facing a six-foot picture window, still boarded for the winter. The only light came from the open door and a small counter lamp Hanson had switched on as he left.

I could tell by the absence of weight on my hip that they had taken my automatic. Not a surprise. I looked down into my shirt pocket, causing a sharp pain to slice through my head. I lay back and waited for the caroming pain in my head to subside.

They carried Kin into the room and placed her on the couch. Hanson blew her a kiss before crossing the room to close the outer door. When he returned, he sank down next to her.

"Here we are, sweetheart. Snug and comfy in our own little Garden of Eden." He did something with his hands that caused Kin to cry out through her gag.

Manzi switched on the only other lamp and looked around with an irritated expression. "It's too damned dark in here," he complained.

Hanson sat up to look around. "Hey, at least the owner kept the power on over the winter. How about you open up that front window, Joey?"

"Why me?" Manzi snorted. "Who put you in charge?"

Trouble in Eden.

Hanson shook his head. "Don't fuck with me, Joey. Just open the goddamn window."

Manzi stared at him, then turned and stalked out of the building, slamming the door.

"Poor Joey," Hanson whispered to Kin. "He's so high strung." He rose and moved two heavy wooden kitchen chairs in front of the couch.

We could hear Manzi outside the window, thumping on the sheet of plywood and cursing at the rain. Hanson laughed.

After a few minutes of struggling, Manzi stormed back into the shack, his hair matted by the rain. "I need a fucking hammer," he snarled.

Hanson was behind the counter looking through the kitchen drawers. He emerged with a coil of clothesline rope. He placed it on one of the chairs, then turned to Manzi. "Hey, Joey, there's a hammer over there in one of those drawers."

Manzi stared at him. "You couldn't get it for me while you were in there?" He was so angry he was shaking.

Hanson uncoiled a six-foot length of rope and sawed through it with a knife he produced from a sheath on his belt.

"I was afraid I might hand it to you the wrong way, give you a sissy fit or something."

"Remember who sent me down here to help you, asshole," Manzi rasped as he stamped into the kitchen.

Hanson grinned as Manzi pulled out each drawer and dumped it onto the floor until he found the hammer. Gripping it and glaring at Hanson, he went outside, slamming the door again.

Hanson bent over Kin. "I really hope the vulgar little man isn't upsetting you, sweetheart. I don't want your memories of our special time together to be spoiled."

Kin made no sound, but her eyes were wild.

"I'm going to sit you in one of those chairs for a while. I hope you don't mind," He cocked his head as if he were listening, then added, "No objection? Good."

He pulled Kin into a standing position. Her bound ankles made it difficult to stand, and she teetered before Hanson put his right arm around her and patted her hip.

"You want to hop to the chair or do you want Uncle Dwayne to carry you?"

Kin mumbled something behind the tape. Her eyes narrowed—rage.

"Hmmm, a honey with a body like yours shouldn't act so rude. Let Uncle Dwayne help you." His hand slid down to cup her rear.

At that moment, the plywood sheet tore free of the window with a rending snap and crashed onto the deck. Hanson turned toward the window. Kin jumped out of his grasp, toppled, and fell. Hanson ignored her as he looked out at Manzi, who was staring in at him. I used that moment to sit up and pull at the tape holding my wrists. There was no give at all. When Hanson turned back to the woman, he noticed me.

"Looky, sweetie. Your big strong man is sitting up and ready to take nourishment."

As he approached me, Hanson changed his stride. I guessed he'd use his right foot. I won that bet and tried to roll with the kick, but I was too immobilized, and it caught me pretty solidly on the left shoulder. Twin blasts of pain rocketed down my arm and up into my head. I hit the floor hard and lay without moving.

Hanson pulled Kin off the floor and plunked her on the chair with no groping. "Your big strong man is still tired. He took another nap."

He roped her securely to the chair.

Manzi shut the outside door and went into the kitchenette, kicking the spilled utensils across the floor. He emerged, drying his hair with a dishtowel.

"If you're finished with your beauty bath, give me a hand," Hanson said.

Without a word, Manzi helped carry and tie me down in the chair next to Kin.

"You both comfy?" Hanson asked us. He turned to Manzi. "Run the van back into town, dump it, and grab the T-bird. The van is big enough to get spotted from the road, but not the car."

Manzi took a step back, his hand slid inside his waterlogged jacket. "There's no way I'm runnin' any more goddamned errands for you," he said, his voice as tight as wire. "You want that van moved, move it your own damn self."

I watched Manzi. It was almost comical except for the look on his face. He was all set to go for his gun like a cowboy in an old Western. They were already divided. For the first time since our capture, I felt real hope.

Hanson dug out a cigarette and lit it, never taking his eyes off Manzi. He sucked in some smoke and blew it toward the other man.

"Tell you what, Joey, let's get this started, then I'll move the van and give our two playmates time to think. You can stand guard." He paused, continuing to watch Manzi. "That okay with you, Joey? Standing guard, I mean."

Manzi's hand reappeared. He peeled off his coat. "Fine," was all he said.

Hanson dragged me around so I faced Kin, then stepped between us, facing her. Leaning over, he stroked her face with his right hand. She pulled away as if it carried an electric charge.

"Oh, sweetheart," he said softly. "We just need some information. If you give it to us, we'll just leave you here and take off. If you don't . . ." He brought his right knee up and then, bending forward, drove the leg straight back. I wasn't expecting it. His foot caught me full in the chest. It knocked the wind out of me and sent me toppling over backwards.

The back of my head slapped against the floor again, spraying bright shards of painful light through my skull. The room darkened as I lay gasping for breath. I tried to open my eyes, but could only blink rapidly. The tape covering my mouth kept me from sucking in the air I desperately needed. Then I caught a glimpse of Manzi's rat face leaning over me and felt the sharp sting of the tape as it was ripped off my mouth. I heard a strange roar echo in the cabin. It took me several seconds to realize that I was making the sound as I sucked deep gulps of air into my lungs. My mind swam as black spots danced across my vision. As they slowly cleared. I became aware of a deep ache in my chest.

They sat me upright again. Hanson mussed my hair and gave me a playful slap in the face. "Did the old man go boom?"

I squinted up at him. "Your . . . name's . . . Hanson," I gasped. "Dwight . . . Hanson . . . right?"

Hanson showed me his teeth. "It's Dwayne, officer. Get your facts straight."

I managed a smile. "You're a . . . dead man . . . Dwight . . . and that's . . . a fact."

Hanson took a drag on his cigarette and laughed aloud, spewing smoke from his mouth. "Is that right?" As he said it, he jabbed the lighted cigarette at my face.

He was fast. I had to give him that. I managed to turn my head just enough for the lighted tip to miss my face, but it caught my left ear. It hurt like hell, distracting me so I couldn't dodge the left hook that followed. It exploded against my right cheek and for the second time in an hour the world burst with a great white flash, and I tumbled into darkness.

I was sitting up again. The right side of my face felt hot and swollen and the jaw ached like it had a bad tooth. My left ear felt as if the cigarette was still burning in it. I opened my eyes. The room wobbled, then righted itself.

Hanson's back was to me. He was standing over Kin and playing what seemed like a child's game.

"Here it comes. Yaaah, rat-tat-tat . . . almost in the mouth, but, noooo. Yeeooww, it's circling . . ."

As his arm came back, I saw another lighted cigarette. He was pretending it was an airplane and buzzing Kin's face with it. Manzi stood to the left, behind the couch, with an irritated expression on his face.

"Stop doing that." It was Kin's voice, anger riding on an undercurrent of terror. They had removed her gag. I knew sadists like Hanson were turned on by the fear.

"You don't want to play?" His voice mocked her. "That makes poor Dwayne feel all rejected and awful."

"Fuck you," Kin snapped, then screamed as Hanson's cigarette airplane crashed into her cheek. She heaved against the ropes, tipped the chair over, and hit the floor hard. She lay there sobbing.

I was witnessing what had happened to Diane. I tugged my arms in the chair. "Hey, Dwight, you got a hard-on yet?"

Hanson's head swiveled slowly until those lifeless eyes crawled over my swollen face.

"Maybe I do, Magill. You want to do something with it?"

I shook my head, which was a mistake. The room danced and I almost vomited. "I'm not into micromanagement," I rasped. "Besides, you probably can't keep it up unless you're beating a woman."

Hanson took his knife from its belt sheath. As he stepped toward me, his arm swung in a sudden arc. I pulled my head back, but the blade tip tore open my left cheek. I felt an immediate throb and a gush of warm blood stream down my face.

"Hey, Dwayne," Manzi interrupted. "You planning on moving that van before you make too much of a mess?"

Hanson straightened and looked from Manzi to me, then back again. Time seemed to be suspended as the sound of Hanson's rapid, shallow breathing served as a counterpoint to the steady wail of the wind outside. Then, as if some internal switch had been thrown, Hanson relaxed, smiled at me and said, "Don't run off. I'll be back, and then we'll have lots more fun."

I could feel the blood dripping from my chin as I gave Hanson a grin. "Can't wait, Dwight. Maybe next time it'll be my turn."

Hanson wiped his knife blade on my sweater before putting it away. Then he showed me those teeth again. "Nicky," he said. "In this game, it's never your turn."

CHAPTER 24

"JOEY." I SOUNDED LIKE A MUMBLE-MOUTHED fighter who had taken too many head shots. I must have looked the part, too. The swelling had almost closed my right eye. The inside of my mouth was raw and filled with the coppery taste of blood. I was aware that the continuous seepage from the knife cut was forging new rivulets down my jaw. My chest felt as if a metal cable was twisted around it, and my ear needed a fire extinguisher.

Like a battered boxer, I knew I was way behind on points, and the only way I could win was by a knockout. As soon as Hanson left with the van, I tried to signal Kin with a wink, but she had retreated somewhere into herself. Then I went after Manzi.

"Joey," I repeated.

He was staring out the picture window with his hands behind him like some gangster general.

"Whaddya want?"

"I want you to keep that crazy bastard away from us."

"Yeah," Manzi said. "I can understand that."

"What do you want from us anyway?"

Manzi lit a cigarette. "Cut the shit. The Ryerson kid."

I tried for a sheepish look but had no way of knowing what came across on my swollen mug. "Help us."

"Like they say, 'let's make a deal,'" he said with a nod.

"We'll give you the kid, and you let us live."

Kin roused herself and stared incredulously at me. "Nick—"

"Shut up," I said. "I'm handling this. What do you say, Joey?"

Manzi nodded a little too enthusiastically. "Sure, I can do that. No problem. I'll meet Dwayne outside, tell him I took care of you, and we'll leave."

You're a piss-poor liar, I thought, but said, "Okay, if I've got your word."

"So, if we've got a deal," Manzi said. "Where the hell is he?"

"I'm hurting, Joey," I said, twisting my body. It wasn't a lie.

"Tough shit. Where is he?"

"All right. We thought he was at this place off Bradford Street, but he's not."

"Yeah, yeah. We followed you there, and I figured that when you came away empty and went to the cops. Dwayne, he wanted to head back there and bust the place up. In broad fucking daylight. So where is the kid?"

"He's staying at another guy's house about a half-mile from there."

I noticed Kin's expression change as I talked.

"What guy? Where's this place?'

"Some friend from A.A. I don't know the street name. I just got directions from that guy at Riley's."

"I saw you talkin' to that shade. Tell me the directions."

I shook my head. "I'll have to draw you a map. Like I say, I don't know streets, only turns."

"Nick," Kin said, her voice shaking. "Don't do this. He's only a boy."

"Screw him," I snapped. "He got himself in trouble. It's our lives or his."

"Shut up, lady," Manzi growled. "We got a deal going here. Listen to your boyfriend, he knows what's what."

"He's not my boyfriend."

"Well, shut up anyway. Look, Magill, how you going to draw me a map tied up? If you think I'm untying you, you're crazy."

I shrugged, winced in pain, and then nodded. "I guess if you're nervous, I understand." I stopped, then began to sob. "I . . . I just don't want to die."

"You coward," Kin barked.

"Lady," Manzi said. "I won't tell you again. Shut your goddamned mouth."

He turned to stare out the window. I wanted to push him, but couldn't afford to overdo it. Better to let the little weasel needle himself. After smoking another cigarette, he glanced at me, then away.

Kin tipped the scale by asking Manzi, "Did Dwayne Hanson ever hurt you?" Without waiting for an answer, she added, "It must be hard working with a man that frightening."

Manzi faced her and actually snorted. "Lady, that whack-job never hurt me, and he certainly don't scare me."

"Oh, sure," Kin said. "I'm sorry."

Manzi dropped his cigarette on the floor and ground it out. "Okay," he said to me. "Here's the deal—I'll free one hand and give you a piece of paper. You draw the map. You try to fuck with me, I'll do you on the spot and give the broad to Hanson to play with. Got that?"

I nodded, then grimaced again. "That's fair." I looked Manzi in the eye. "Thanks, Joey."

He looked away, then walked into the kitchenette and pawed through the materials dumped on the floor.

A minute later, he came back with a spiral notebook and a plastic pen.

Shit, I didn't want plastic.

He dragged a folding table with a two-foot square top over to me and placed the pen and notebook on it. Pulling out a pocketknife, he cut my right hand free. "Draw the map," he said.

I picked up the pen, praying that it had been stored point-up all winter. Using as little pressure as I could, I dragged the pen across the page. It left no line. Dropping it on the table, I said, "It's out of ink. But I got one, Joey."

When I began to reach into my shirt pocket, Manzi sprang forward with the still-open pocket knife. "Lemme see that."

I took my hand away, and Manzi pulled the metal pen from my pocket.

"You just twist it to get the point out," I said.

"I know how to use a fucking pen, shithead." He dropped it on the table. "Make the map. Your time's running out."

I put pen to paper. "I'll start at Riley's, 'cause that's the way I know."

He faced me, looking down with his open knife still in his hand. When I glanced up at him, I saw the butt of his gun, still snapped into his shoulder holster.

"You go down the street here, turn right, then go two blocks and turn right—oh, shit." The pen slipped from my fingers and fell to the floor. Manzi stepped back.

"Sorry. My arm hurts like crazy from that bastard pounding on me." I tried to grab for the pen on the floor, but it was out of my reach.

"Can you get that, Joey? I'm strapped into the chair."

"Asshole," Manzi muttered as he picked up the pen and handed it to me.

"Thanks."

"Draw the fucking map."

I began drawing again and continued my narration. "Here, you go left and up two streets, but—and this is the tricky part—you have to cut back—" I suddenly doubled over, moaning. As I did, I palmed the pen.

Kin wailed, "Oh God, is he all right?"

Manzi glanced at her.

"Oh no," I whined. "I dropped the stupid pen again. I'm really sorry."

"Jesus Christ, you're a fucking joke."

"It rolled under the chair, I think."

He squatted down, then looked up at me. "Where the hell did it . . ."

That was as far as he got before I drove the pen into his throat.

Joey Manzi gave a strangled cry, dropped his pocketknife and grabbed at the pen protruding from his neck. As he did that, I threw myself, chair and all, into him.

The impact took both of us to the floor.

Manzi grabbed at his throat, then pulled his hand away and stared, wild-eyed, at what looked like a red glove. With my free hand, I struck at the pen to drive it deeper, but missed and hit his jaw. The blow seemed to snap him out of his panic. I felt him going for his gun. He lurched and struggled. I could feel him twisting free. I punched him again, but had no leverage. He got his hand into his coat and on the gun. I punched him again, knowing that if he got that gun out, we were both dead.

"Nick!"

I glanced up, fearing Hanson had returned.

Kin yelled, "Here," and kicked Manzi's open knife toward me. As it caromed off his shoulder, I felt him pull his gun free. I hammered him once with my fist in the middle of his face, then grabbed for the knife. As my hand closed on its handle, I heard the gun's safety click off. I blindly swung the knife and stabbed him—again and again and again—until I heard Kin screaming.

"He's dead, Nick. Stop, please stop."

I rolled off him and cut myself free, then grabbed his gun and ran to the door and eased it open. There was no sign of Dwayne Hanson. I dragged another chair over and wedged it under the doorknob.

"Cut me loose," Kin shouted.

I hurried over to her and set to work on the tape and ropes.

"Sorry to leave you there, but I was afraid Hanson would walk in on us."

She stood up and backed away from what was left of Joey Manzi, saying, "It's okay. It's okay. Please, let's get out of here." Then she looked at me in horror. "My god, you're covered in blood."

I looked down at my hands, sweater, and jeans. They looked as if I had bathed in red dye. "I hope this son-of-a-bitch isn't HIV positive," I said, pulling off the sweater and throwing it to the side.

Kin looked horrified. "Are you okay?"

I felt nauseous and weak and my body ached as if it had just fallen off a cliff. I said, "Don't worry. He didn't cut me. I'm fine."

I saw my automatic on the kitchen counter. I slid it into the holster on my left hip. My cell phone was nowhere in sight. I looked at Manzi's body. "It would have been a lot worse if you hadn't kicked me that knife. I'm just sorry you had to see him die."

She nodded, then went to an armoire at the foot of the bunk beds. "There are some old shirts in here and a coat if you want to get out of those clothes."

The coat was a little tight, but I could wear it. The black fabric of my jeans made it difficult to tell what kind of stain ran from knee to cuff.

"Okay," I said. "Let's get out of here and get some police."

"What if he comes along while we're walking on the road?"

"You get off the road and hide."

She frowned. "What are you going to do?"

I hoisted Manzi's Glock. "I'm going to shoot the bastard."

CHAPTER 25

KIN STOOD BEHIND ME as I opened the cabin door. A blast of wind made me blink as I looked outside. No sign of the T-bird. The packed dirt drive bisected a low dune covered with beach grass that ended in a roadside barrier of scrub pine and stunted oak. I started to step onto the tiny porch when something moved in the grass. I froze, then reached back to Kin.

"Wait. Stay inside."

"Why?" she asked, leaning forward.

Something flickered left to right in the grass. The wind was blowing right to left. "Get back," I yelled and pushed her back into the shack.

She yelped and grabbed at the top bunk to keep from going down. At the same instant, a splinter of wood from the doorframe hit me above my left eye. It was followed immediately by a crack of gunfire.

"Hanson. Get down," I shouted as I tumbled inside, slammed the door, and tackled her. She gasped as we sprawled on the floor. I was on top of her when the another bullet tore through the door, followed by three more. A small photo on the far wall shattered and I felt another piece of wood strike my leg.

I rolled off her onto my knees with the Glock pointed at the perforated door. There was no sound except the wind buffeting the cabin. I grabbed Kin by the arm, pulled her into the kitchen, and dumped her against the refrigerator. I kept looking from the door to the picture window for any sign of Hanson. Kin was crying softly, but I had no idea if it was from fear or because I had hurt her. It didn't matter as long as she was safe.

Then, over the moan of the wind, I heard a car engine start and rev. I left the kitchen and opened the front door. I could hear the whine of a transmission straining in reverse. Hanson had parked on the drive next to the road. And now he was getting away. I ran down the narrow drive, keeping low. I heard car tires squeal on pavement as the T-bird accelerated. I stopped and straightened, my gun hanging in my hand. Goddamn it, the bastard was gone. That infuriating thought was suddenly knocked out of the way by one much worse. I turned and sprinted back to the shack.

"Is he gone?" was Kin's first question when I burst through the door.

"Yeah." I took her hand. "Come on, we have to go now."

"What's the matter?"

I took her to the door. "Come on, " I repeated. "I'll tell you on the way."

She resisted my pull. "On the way where?"

"To Riley's," I said. I stepped onto the porch. "Hurry, for Christ's sake."

"What's the matter with you? Hanson's gone."

"Yeah—to Riley's. We have to find a phone and get some cops over there, before he slaughters more people."

CHAPTER 26

I IMMEDIATELY REGRETTED wearing boots. After we had jogged for about a half-mile, I could feel the soggy leather raising a blister on my ankle. The heavy rain had returned, and we were both soaked as we searched in vain for an occupied house. The few at this end of town were still closed for the season, and the only car that came by swerved around us when we tried to flag it down. Apparently, our sodden appearance and my swollen, bloodstained face weren't reassuring.

Finally, as we came over a low rise, we saw a motel with a lighted vacancy sign ahead on the right. We broke into a run. As we reached the entrance, a cab was about to pull out toward town. I sprinted toward it, yelling and waving my arms. The driver stopped and rolled down his window.

"You want a cab?"

I stopped next to him. "I sure as hell do. But I need to use your cell phone first—it's an emergency."

"Sorry, bud. My phone doesn't work on this end of town."

"Just a second." I turned to Kin. "Use the phone inside. Send the cops—Manny Batista, if you can get him—to Riley's. I'll meet them there."

"Wait," she gasped. "I want to go with you."

I placed my hand on her cheek. "Stay here, please. I'll see you in a while."

She frowned but nodded. I climbed into the rear of the cab.

The driver, a young man with an uncertain beard and a ponytail, wore a slightly worried expression. "Sorry to ask this, mister," he said, eyeing my battered face and ill-fitting jacket. "You got any money? No offense."

"None taken," I said, as I yanked out my wallet and showed him some cash. "Just get me to Dodge Street, fast. There's a twenty dollar tip if you need to break traffic laws."

The driver gave me a crooked grin.

"Hang on, mister. For twenty I'll have you there yesterday."

The cab's tires shrieked against the wet pavement. I looked back. Kin gave a tentative wave, then turned and ran into the motel.

As the cab turned onto Dodge Street, I saw a gray sedan parked below the stairs to Riley's. Beyond it, I could see the tail of Manzi's T-bird. The cab's old windshield wipers only smeared the heavy rain, making it difficult to see if the cars were occupied.

"Stop behind the gray car," I said, handing the cabbie his money.

When the cab swung to the side of the road, I saw a body lying at the foot of the porch steps.

"Holy shit," the driver yelped as he slammed on the brakes. "There's a guy down out there."

"Take off, go to the cops," I said, then got out and sprinted to the rear of the gray sedan. I could hear the whine of the cab backing away.

There was no movement from the house. Staying low, I edged along the street-side of the car until I had a clear view of the man on the ground. Aiming my gun at the building, I duck-walked to him and checked for a pulse. Nothing. I recognized him as one of the two FBI agents who were looking for me. A glance at his concave left temple told me to stop wasting time. Through the driving rain, I could see no movement from the porch. I took a deep breath and sprinted up the steps.

The shorter, stockier agent lay sprawled on his back by the front door, shot in the face. Past him, just inside the door, lay an old man with a severe facial contusion. I took a peek inside and saw Johnson with a towel pressed against his own chest, propped in a corner. A baseball bat lay in the middle of the floor. Johnson was conscious and gestured weakly at me. I moved to his side.

"Where is he?" I asked as I panned the hallway and stairs with my gun.

"Shit," Johnson whispered, "You look like shit. 'Bout time you got here." He gestured at the bat. "I gave that asshole a good lick, but he's long gone. Out back, I think. I been a little preoccupied here."

I examined the chest wound. It was bad, but high and to the right. His breathing sounded clear enough for me to hope the bullet had missed his lung.

"Hang on. The cops are on the way," I said.

"Fuckin' wonderful," he said, then closed his eyes.

I pointed. "He went out that way?"

Johnson's eyelids struggled to half-mast and nodded. "After Jimmy. Man, you called it."

"I'm going to nail his ass," I told him. "Don't you die on me."

His eyes closed. He showed me a faint smile and nodded again.

I moved through the house. As I stepped out of the back door, I heard three shots in rapid succession. Low caliber—probably a .22. I ran up the hill, found a path, and limped as fast as I could in the direction of the shots.

The path through a grove of scrub pines and young oaks emptied into a cemetery. I had heard no more gunshots—maybe there was still time. Fifty yards ahead, a blur of movement through the rain caught my eye—someone moving away, dropping out of my line of sight. Hanson, I thought, and started after him when I noticed what looked like a sack of clothing leaning against a tombstone, straight ahead of me.

"Oh, Jesus, no," I said aloud. I wiped my good eye, hoping it wasn't what I knew it was.

"Damn it, goddamn it," I swore into the rain as I walked to the boy's body.

Jimmy Ryerson sat upright, leaning back on a sunken gravestone. His head, tipped back, rested on its rough edge. Rain had puddled in his brown eyes as he stared through the water into another world. His mouth gaped open, as if in surprise. A deep, ragged cut had opened his throat and released his blood into his sweatshirt. He still wore the ponytail and he looked too damned young to be dead. I shrugged off the coat I had taken from the shack and gently spread it over his face. I gritted my teeth. That fucker had taken another one.

Then I noticed the knife in the boy's right hand—as if he had cut his own throat. This had to be Hanson's idea of confusing the investigation. I shook my head, amazed this skank was still walking around loose. It was an insult to Diane and all the others he had killed.

I turned and started to follow Hanson. Then my training kicked in. Get within range—without being seen. Make sure you can take your shot. Do it on your terms.

I was betting that Hanson would not go back to Riley's for the T-bird. Not after the O.K. Corral he had pulled back there. He was smart enough to head for the road and steal another car as soon as he could. I ran to my left, through a patch of briars and into more scrub pines and oaks. I pushed through the branches, holding my left arm in front of my face, but a limb skidded under my wrist and snapped free, striking me in the corner of my swollen right eye. Pain flashed through my head, but my rage kept me going.

I broke out of the trees onto a short slope leading down to the street and slid down the grass and sand. I landed in a puddle seconds after a cruiser sped past, going in the direction of Riley's. Scrambling to my feet, I moved to my right toward a curve in the road twenty yards away. I ran along the grass at the edge of the street until I reached a large pine tree that grew out of a hedge enclosing a yard. At the tree, I heard a crunching sound over the drumming of the rain. It took me a few seconds to recognize it as the sound of someone walking with heavy boots on shells or gravel. I stepped behind the tree just as Hanson strutted out onto the street, with barely a glance behind him, and walked away as if he didn't have a care in the world. Because he probably didn't. Psychopaths don't feel those emotions that hold the rest of us in check.

I moved quickly past the tree and along the hedge until I was within twenty feet of him. I aimed my gun at his back and wanted to put a permanent stop to that insolent swagger. As much as I was justified—even picturing Diane, my wife, my first love, dead in that chair, I couldn't pull the trigger. I had broken a lot of laws in the past two days, but I couldn't join Hanson's murder club. Instead, I stepped into the street and yelled, "Dwight!"

CHAPTER 27

Hanson stopped but didn't turn, his hands rammed into his duster pockets. I had no doubt that he knew who was calling him.

"Yo, Dwight," I repeated. "Remove your hands from your pockets and place them on top of your head."

Hanson's hands stayed in his coat as he slowly turned his head and looked back at me. I could see him noting the wind blowing the rain in my face and my right eye almost swollen shut. He showed me a thin smile. "Hey, Nicky, you got me, okay?"

Slowly his left hand came out of the coat. He turned his palm over, showing me it was empty, then placed it on his head, at the same time turning his body so that he stood sideways to me.

As a kid, I had read that Doc Holliday always turned sideways during gunfights to make himself a narrower target. This fool had watched too many westerns.

"Dwight, you have trouble with English? I said both hands. Show me your right hand and show it to me empty." I took a half-step forward.

Hanson nodded his head. "I'm doing it, officer. That spook back there whaled me with a baseball bat. It messed my right shoulder up so it's hard for me to move too quick."

"It's too bad he didn't take your head off, asshole. Now, stop the whining and do it." Then I added, "By the way, that spook, as you call him, is going to live to I.D. you."

Hanson winced. I wasn't sure if pulling his right hand out of the coat hurt or if he was upset that Johnson was still alive. He showed me what I assumed was his idea of a defeated, pathetic expression. It only made his horse face uglier. "Look, you got me," he said. "There's one more gun in my shoulder rig. I can pull it and toss it. I don't want to get shot for nothing."

"Shooting a piece of shit like you would never be for nothing," I said. "Okay, take the weapon out. By the butt, using your left hand. Do it just like you're in a slow-motion movie."

"Yes, sir."

He awkwardly worked the gun loose, holding it by the butt, barrel down. I pointed to the grass at the side of the road. "Toss it over there . . . easy. I'm betting that's the gun that killed Diane Zeolla."

"You knew her?" Hanson asked as he began to swing the gun back and forth. "So sorry for your loss."

"Throw the gun," I snarled. I could feel the rage building.

"Yessir," he said, and tossed the gun toward the side of the road.

It landed in the tall grass.

"I got a sap. You want me to toss that, too?"

"You're a smart guy, Dwight. You won't have any trouble understanding what's going on when they slip that needle into your vein."

He smirked. "There's no capital punishment in Massachusetts."

"You killed two federal officers, genius. That's another ball game."

Hanson frowned at that. "I'm getting the sap out of my pocket now," he said. "I'm going real slow." Using his left hand, he tugged the blackjack into view, then added, "You close to Miz Zeolla?"

I didn't respond.

"Ain't it a shame what happens to nice people in this world."

I clenched my teeth to bite off my anger. "Throw. The. Sap."

He smirked and began swinging it the way he had swung the shoulder gun. I watched as his right hand slid from view. Two dead federal officers who probably carried Glocks, but he had only shown me one Glock. I thought of Diane and the others this creature had killed. He deserved to die, and I wanted to let him make the play. But that wasn't the way I was taught. All I needed to do was take him in.

"Hanson, don't—" It was as far as I got when he released the blackjack, sending it through the air. As he did that, Hanson grabbed the other gun in his pocket, twisted it up, and shot through his coat.

It was the kind of move that worked—in the movies. Shooting for accuracy is hard enough under optimal conditions, but through fabric, while twisting, without aiming—as I said, only in Hollywood.

His bullet missed. Mine tore through his left side and into his chest. He staggered sideways as if he had lost his balance before his legs folded and he dropped to a sitting position, legs splayed. The smirk was still on his face until he looked up at me. Then his eyes widened in surprise, and he fell onto his back.

I walked to where he sprawled face-up in the driving rain. As much a victim of violence as all the people he had stalked and killed. Only this time, he had done it to himself. When I reached him, he blinked at me and opened his mouth to speak, but a low, rattling groan escaped on a froth of blood and took his life with it. His eyes, empty before, looked bottomless now.

I had done what I promised Diane I would do—I had evened the score. But I didn't feel relief. Instead, I felt damaged in some dark part of my soul.

The rain pounded his body mercilessly, as if it were trying to cleanse him of his sins. It was a hopeless task, but I was still watching the process when the first cruiser skidded to a stop beside me.

CHAPTER 28

"Okay," Manny Batista said, almost apologetically. "Let's run through it one more time."

Batista was built like a beer keg, with a round, smiling face that seemed to sit directly on his thick shoulders. He wore his hair short on the sides, but longer in the back in a style that reminded me of the haircut favored by some Boston wiseguys. An onyx ear post winked in his left ear.

I went through it once more, from Diane's call to my shooting of Dwayne Hanson. My only omissions were the discoveries of Diane's and Mookie Davis's bodies. Batista checked his notes against what I had told him the first three times, nodding to himself. Five hours had elapsed since the killing of Hanson. It seemed as if Diane's call had come a month ago.

Lieutenant Richard Souza had sat in on the second interview. He was a tall, narrow man whose gaunt appearance was exaggerated by a navy-blue suit and an almost shaved head. His interrogation technique consisted of interrupting me with sarcastic remarks. An hour into it, I had stopped to announce that I was through talking until I called my lawyer. That had peeved Souza, but he had to allow the call.

My attorney, Dexter Brohanon, was famous for his courtroom skills and political clout. First, he gave me hell for making any statement at all. He told me not to say anything more until he flew down in approximately an hour. Then he had asked to speak to Lieutenant Souza. I watched Souza's perpetual sneer tighten and his dark-eyed gaze hop rapidly around the room. He hung up and stalked out of the room shortly thereafter.

Batista had come in fifteen minutes ago. I liked him, so I had decided to talk to him. Now, he tipped back in his metal chair and sighed. "I'm satisfied it was a righteous shoot. I would have liked it better if you were a little more forthcoming with our desk sergeant, but, as you've noted, he ain't exactly the kind of guy that invites intimacy." He made a dismissive gesture with his hand. "From what your old partner and another guy I know from B.P.D. tell me, this Hanson was a psycho piece of shit who should have been flushed a long time ago."

I nodded. "Smooth-talking devils, aren't they?"

Batista laughed, showing me a gold molar. "Yeah, and always politically correct."

We both chuckled, then I leaned toward Batista. "What's next? We just waiting for Brohanon to arrive?"

Batista shrugged. "Yeah, you'll probably want to have your attorney present when we take a formal statement for the charging package. That's just a formality, as you know. I doubt we're looking for anything but justifiable homicide for Hanson or Manzi."

"You doubt?"

"Well, on the phone, your attorney sort of tied a knot in my lieutenant's tail. He may try to get even by dragging his feet, but . . ." He trailed off, then scratched his chin. "It's okay with me and the D.A., but there is a Justice Department guy here who's been thumping and bumping, wanting to see you. Got kind of an attitude, so

I told him you'd want to wait for your lawyer to arrive. He wasn't happy to hear that. This guy thinks he's a real hard-on."

"When I was on the force," I said, "I always enjoyed being demeaned by the Feebs. I can't wait to see him. This will be a blast from the past."

"Mr. Magill, please be seated. I am Agent Harold Holbrook."

He was sitting at a gray metal table so that the light from the wire-mesh window behind him kept his face in shadow. The same light would be in my eyes as we talked. It was a trick I had used many times when I was on the job. Brown-framed reading glasses sat on his thick, hooked nose as he read the initial police report.

Holbrook appeared to be an older clone of the two dead officers—except there was something familiar about him. He was neatly uniformed in a gray suit, with a snow-white shirt and royal blue tie. His square head was topped with very short, neatly parted hair—like a generic fed. Maybe that was why it seemed as if I had met him.

When I was seated, Holbrook placed his elbows on the table and made a steeple with his two index fingers. His blue eyes studied the structure, then focused on me.

"All right, Mr. Magill," he said sternly. "You killed Mr. Dwayne Hanson and Mr. Joseph Manzi. We agree on that, yes?"

"No."

He frowned at me. "No?"

"No. I'd never call those scum 'mister,' but other than that, your statement seems superficially correct."

"Superficially?"

"Yes. I defended my life and the life of Jean McKinnon. Hanson and Manzi were professional killers."

"So it would appear. The question is whether the killing of Mr. Hanson could have been avoided."

"Why? Are you a relative?"

Holbrook removed his glasses and pinched the bridge of his nose. "Obviously not, Mr. Magill. And being sarcastic will not help to resolve the matter of this death. You are aware that we may charge you with his homicide."

I laughed aloud. "Look, Mr. Holbrook, let's understand each other. I shot an armed man as he was discharging his weapon at me. He had just murdered a nineteen-year-old boy and two of your men. Then there's Johnson, Diane Zeolla, that old man at Riley's, and the attempt on Robbie Atkinson's life, as well as the abduction of Ms. McKinnon and myself. If you think you can hang anything but self-defense on me, take your best shot."

Holbrook stared at me, then returned to examining his fingers. "Maybe you're right, Mr. Magill," he said after a few moments. "But you've compromised an ongoing investigation with your Lone Ranger tactics. Concealing evidence—that is something that we could pursue."

I wondered what they knew. "Really, Agent Holbrook? Just what ongoing investigation have I impeded?"

"I'm not free to discuss it, but you have definitely muddied the waters."

"You boys sure do have muddy water, but I'm not the one stirring up the sludge."

His eyes narrowed. "Meaning what?"

"Meaning that because Jimmy Ryerson was Jonathan Price's step-son, and took photos of him, this involves Price, which in turn means it involves Frankie Fallon. You guys have been dying to bring Fallon down for years. This boy had something to do with all this, but you guys screwed up by letting Hanson run loose."

"We did not even know that Hanson existed," Holbrook snapped. "We would never—"

"Please," I said, standing up. "There have been too many coincidences. Whenever Hanson and Manzi were around, so were your boys. Someone had to be feeding the same information to both sides. That's a real messy situation, and I think you're down here trying to do damage control by attempting to intimidate me. I—" I stopped and stared at Holbrook as if I were seeing him for the first time. I walked to the door and switched on the overhead light. Holbrook jumped up.

"Sit down, now!"

I crossed the room and leaned across the desk. Holbrook pushed himself back in his chair.

"It's you in the third photograph, isn't it, you son of a bitch? I didn't make the connection at first, because your hair was a little shorter and you were wearing sunglasses." I grinned at Holbrook. "You've got Price by the balls and you're using him to bring Fallon down."

Holbrook slammed his hand on the table. "Watch yourself, Magill, or you'll be locked up until this is over."

"Look at yourself. Backlighting, hiding in shadows—cut the dramatic bullshit, Holbrook. There are too many dead people piled up to hide in the dark. You goddamn clowns are going to use Price to bring Fallon's crew down and, in return, you're going to let that oily bastard disappear into your witness protection program. Price has to be the one responsible for all this carnage, and he's got a pass to get out of jail free, doesn't he?"

Holbrook had begun to shake his head before I was finished. As he started to speak, I saw a flash of fear disappear behind a blink.

"That's all preposterous. You have no idea of what trouble this kind of wild specula—" He stopped as the door opened and Dexter Brohanon stepped into the room.

Brohanon's arrival was the only thing that kept me from punching Holbrook. Dexter Brohanon had that kind of effect on many people. At six-five, two-thirty, with a mane of pale blond hair framing a face weathered by years of ocean sailing, he had a powerful physical presence. Add to that his sure grasp of the subtleties of the law and his knowledge of the location of many political skeletons, and he became a lawyer people not only noticed and respected, but also feared.

"Agent Holbrook," he said without expression. "It's nice to see you again. Unfortunately, my client can't talk with you anymore. We have to make a formal statement and arrange for his release." Brohanon waved me toward the door.

Holbrook looked as if he were trying to swallow a lobster whole.

"You'll need the time to arrange all the funerals your Judas has caused," I said to him.

A string of curses followed us out of the room.

CHAPTER 29

I HAD GIVEN MY STATEMENT, as had Kin. Now we sat on a bench in a hallway near the front desk. The constant crackle of radio transmissions from patrol cars and the ringing of telephones shielded our conversation.

"Your Mr. Brohanon is certainly impressive," Kin said. "I'm amazed at how he's taken charge. Before he came, I was scared to death I'd say the wrong thing. Officer Souza spent almost two hours trying to get me to say something incriminating about you."

"Yeah, Brohanon apparently chewed him out a bit over the phone. You were a safe way for him to get even."

She looked at me. "I didn't tell him anything except what they tried to do to us—that monster Hanson, and Manzi." She looked both ways and lowered her voice. "I—I didn't mention Mookie at all. I knew you'd get in trouble if I did, so . . . "

I smiled at her and squeezed her hand. "Thanks. If the cops are any good, they'll tie Jimmy to Mookie, and ballistics will tie Hanson to the kill."

"Poor Jimmy," she said.

I nodded. "Yeah, a terrible waste of life. I don't know why he thought he could go up against that kind of power and get away with it."

Kin stared across the hall in silence, then turned to me again. "What I think it is—beyond adolescent misjudgment—is the paradox of the alcoholic."

"What paradox?"

"Active alcoholics are full of self-hate but want desperately to be important—to have the world love them—to convince themselves they're not as powerless as they feel. When a person acts that way, we say, 'He or she is the piece of shit the world revolves around.' I guess Jimmy wanted to validate himself. He wanted to do something so heroic it would prove that he wasn't as bad as he felt. Does that make sense?"

"It makes me think of that kid with the wax wings in Greek mythology who flew too close to the sun."

"Icarus?"

I nodded. "Jimmy probably knew what he was doing was dangerous, but he couldn't not do it."

"But his wings didn't melt," Kin said, tears running down her cheeks. "Dwayne Hanson cut them off."

Two hours later, we stood on the sidewalk. It was dark, the rain had stopped, but a raw wind whistled between the buildings, carrying dampness from the harbor. Brohanon had kept Holbrook at bay and arranged to have them release me on personal recognizance, pending a hearing in two days. I had expected some sort of relief from all this. Instead, I felt numb.

Kin yawned and rubbed her eyes. "Boy," she said, looking up at me, "you're a fun guy to hang around with."

I managed a smile. "I never had this much fun until I met you."

She smiled back, then pushed up her sleeve and tipped her watch so it was illuminated by the nearby streetlight. "I don't know what your plans are, but after all this insanity, I could really use a meeting."

"You mean A.A.?"

"I don't mean the Police Benevolent Association," she said.

When I didn't respond, she shrugged. "A tiny attempt at humor. Sorry. Yes, I mean A.A. I don't know if you want to come along." She dug a meeting list out of her purse and stepped toward the light. "There's a meeting an hour from now," she said, smiling. "It's a short walk from here. What do you say?"

I shrugged. It felt as if my chest and shoulders were filled with cement. Walking would feel good after sitting for all those hours. My exhaustion had departed two hours ago, leaving me edgy and alert. If she's going, I thought, what the hell else am I going to do?

What I said was, "They don't mind if non-alcoholics come?"

"It's an open meeting," she said. "That means that you can come. There's only one thing—no, two things I ask of you."

"What's that?"

"Number one, try to keep an open mind."

"I'll try. I know I have some problems with this alcoholism thing. What's number two?"

"Don't shoot anyone."

"I can't," I said. "They still have my gun."

We bought sandwiches on the way to the church where the meeting was. Entering through a side door, we descended worn steps into a large basement room. Rows of chairs faced a wooden podium flanked by two banners listing the twelve steps. I was too nervous to read them, and Kin didn't seem to mind when I wanted to sit at the rear of the hall, against the wall.

"It feels safer," I muttered, feeling the need to explain.

She shrugged and gave me one of her dazzling smiles. Why did this please her?

The room began to fill. I was amazed at how healthy so many of the people looked. Sure, there were a few who looked like they had been dropped and dragged—even a couple of guys who might have had a couple of snorts before they showed up—but so many of them were joking and laughing. I suddenly felt a deep sadness. Why couldn't have my father gotten sober? I turned to Kin and whispered, "Is it okay for people to show up here if they've been drinking?"

"Sure. All you need is a desire to stop drinking."

"Even if you can't do it yet?"

"That's right."

I looked around the hall. "Huh," I said.

Kin put a hand on my shoulder and left it there. "And that's only the beginning."

"What happens if one of your close friends in A.A. goes back to drinking?" I asked.

"That happens," she said. "You can only offer them your hand, and hope they make it back to recovery. Sometimes they do, sometimes they slide away."

"Damn," I said glancing at her. "Doesn't that make you want to step back and not get involved?"

"There's no place to step back to. We come to A.A. because it's the last house on the block. Usually, it's that or death, jail, dementia, whatever. And it's pretty hard not to bond with people when you share such personal details in meetings."

"Like what?"

"You're about to find out," she said.

In the front of the room, a woman stepped to a podium and asked for a moment of silence. Then she made a few housekeeping announcements and read some passages from what I took to be A.A. literature. I was dozing off when the woman invited a guy named Bruce to come up to the podium. She sat down, and he started to speak.

Bruce introduced himself as an alcoholic. He was about my age, and he was wearing a suit, as if he had come there from work. He was a lawyer, and for decades he had "practiced both law and alcoholism," as he put it, before getting sober five years ago. What followed was an account of the kinds of horror shows I had experienced as a kid and as a cop—car accidents, brawls, domestic violence. At one point he stood there in front of about twenty-five people, talking about hitting his wife when he was drunk, tears leaking from his eyes. I was stunned. The story didn't end there. He was fired from his own firm and nearly disbarred, but not even these events had motivated him to stop drinking.

I felt a slow burn of familiar anger. This is exactly what I could never understand about my father. *You destroy everything and everyone around you, and you still aren't willing to stop? Give me a break.*

Bruce talked about trying to quit drinking, but he never made it through a single day. He said he had only one tool in his toolbox: booze. If he felt happy or angry or sad, he drank. He didn't have any other coping skills, so when he felt anything, any kind of feeling, he physically craved alcohol. This confused me. The physical craving I'd witnessed was when my father ran out of booze, pacing the kitchen, sweat breaking out on his face. It didn't seem to relate to his emotions except to provoke fury.

When Bruce's life was circling the drain, he decided to kill himself by throwing himself in front of a truck. Crouching in a ditch by the side of a two-lane road in the dark, he waited for a good-sized vehicle to come along. But he was three sheets to the wind, and he passed out in the ditch, only to wake up there in the morning with a nightmare hangover. "I even failed at suicide," he said, laughing.

His audience broke into peals of laughter. I thought it was funny too, but it was also stupid and pathetic. Were they laughing at him or with him?

That day Bruce realized that he wanted to live. He couldn't go on drinking, and he didn't know how to stop. He asked his sober cousin to take him to an A.A. meeting, and he hadn't had a drink since that day. He went on about "the tools of A.A." and "finding a higher power" and a lot of other things I didn't comprehend. His face was radiant when he described his sober career as a public defender who specialized in helping alcoholic clients. He was divorced, but he had made a sincere apology to his wife and kids. He called it an "amends." They had not forgiven him, and he was trying to accept that. "In their shoes, I probably wouldn't forgive me either," he said. "But in sobriety I've had to learn how to forgive myself, or I'd be drinking again."

"So, what did you think?" Kin asked. We were in the Porsche, driving back to Hyannis after the A.A. meeting.

"It was interesting to see what goes on in a meeting. That part was good."

"But?"

My grip tightened on the steering wheel. "I have questions, but they haven't gotten to the verbal stage yet. Bruce's story stirred up a lot of old emotions."

"I can imagine. You were on the receiving end of alcoholic abuse, and here's this room full of alkies laughing about things they did when they were drunk. You were like Alice going through the looking glass."

"That's about right," I said. "I didn't always feel like laughing along."

"Have you heard of Al-Anon, Nick?"

"Diane mentioned it in relation to clients once in a while. It's for people who live with alcoholics, as I understand it."

"Yes, and for anyone who's affected by someone else's addiction, even in the past. I go to Al-Anon meetings periodically myself. They help me detach—to not try to be in charge of what other people do." She was silent for a moment. "My sister is still out there—using. Al-Anon helps me live with that and not keep trying to rescue her."

I didn't respond, and after a few moments Kin spoke. "Didn't you say that you have an alcoholic brother?"

I was strangling the steering wheel again. "Yeah. I don't even know if my brother is alive or dead," I snapped. "I don't even know if I care."

"Al-Anon might be helpful," she said.

The rest of the trip was silent. I used that silence to chew on an idea. It meant doing something that went against everything I had been taught and believed. It also meant putting myself a lot farther outside the law than I was now. By the time we reached Hyannis, I had made my decision.

I swung the Porsche into her driveway and parked. Her car was still at the resort. When I asked if she wanted to get it, she shook her head, saying it was too late and she was too tired. We climbed out of the car and walked to her front door.

"Where are you—" she started to ask.

I touched a finger to her lips. "I'm going to Boston tonight. There's something I need to do."

"It's awfully late and you're exhausted and injured. Couldn't you do it tomorrow? I have a couch."

I craved a good night's sleep at a cellular level, but I shook my head. "I have to do this tonight or it might not get done. I'll call you tomorrow. Maybe we could have dinner or something."

"What do you have to do tonight?"

"I need to see a snake about a fox," I said.

CHAPTER 30

Fɪꜰᴛʏ ᴍɪɴᴜᴛᴇꜱ ʟᴀᴛᴇʀ, I was on the Southeast Expressway, the Boston skyline directly ahead of me. Since I left the force, I had not enjoyed visiting the city, probably because I had grown up there and then worked in the clutch of its dirty fist of poverty and crime. The city's wealthy power brokers squatted in their suburban estates or in harbor-view condos where they began the day watching the sunrise over the ocean. At night, they could pretend that the city lights were the jewels of their industry rather than the warning flares of their urban greed. Jonathan Price was probably home right now, sleeping like a baby.

My years as a Boston homicide detective had scarred me in ways I hadn't realized until I was out of the life and out of the city. Returning to Boston for me was like re-entering Dante's Inferno. As the skyline loomed larger, I remembered a line from Dante:

> *The soles of them were all on fire, whence pain*
> *Made their joints quiver and thrash with such*
> *   strong throes,*
> *They'd have snapped withies and hempen ropes*
> *   in twain . . .*

I couldn't even recall why I had picked up the book, or what a withy was, but the passage had seized my attention. I quoted it once to Art and added, "These are the goddamned people we see every day." Art had just looked at me for a moment, then replied, "What does this Dante say about people who aren't cops?" We had laughed for a good five minutes.

I took the exit for South Boston. My family had lived in a tough neighborhood in Southie, near the Dorchester line. I learned to fight early and, by the time I was a teenager, I had enough of a reputation that I was able to walk the streets with a minimum of interference. My brother, Darren, had chosen another route to acceptance—alcohol and drugs. By age fourteen, he was using them, selling them, and hanging with mob-wannabe street punks.

It was our drunk of a father who pushed me headlong into Carmine "Snake" Antonelli.

By the tenth grade, Antonelli was sporting the nickname, "Snake." Some kids said it was because of his quick and savage attacks on those who fought him. Others claimed the nickname originated when his classmates glimpsed his physical endowments in the boys' locker room. Whenever he was asked about it, Antonelli smirked and said nothing.

As I heard it, Patrick Magill was lurching home from the Pine Tree Tap on a hot June evening when he collided with the eighteen-year-old Antonelli, just as Antonelli was rounding a corner with two friends. The impact knocked the old man to the sidewalk and bounced Antonelli against a telephone pole. My father staggered to his feet and threw a wild right at the startled teenager. By chance, the drunken swing caught Antonelli high on the left cheek, causing him to stumble backwards. Humiliated in front of his friends, Antonelli was on my father with a series of devastating punches. My father went down, unconscious before he landed in the gutter. Only a drunk's luck kept his head from hitting the curb. Antonelli walked away without a backward glance.

Later that night, an emergency room doctor had assured me that my father would recover from the beating. I left my sad-eyed mother at the hospital and went out to find Antonelli, because in my world at the time, that is what a man did.

I had found Antonelli at a bar called The Grotto. He was outside, lounging against the building with his two friends, looking cool. We had gone through junior high and high school together, but had never talked or had any contact with each other. I walked up and called him out for what he had done to my father. Antonelli waved his two boys back as they came off the wall. They resumed their studied poses.

"Your old man called it," Antonelli said. "He punched me in the face."

I had gestured toward the alley across the street. "Well, now I'm going to have to do the same thing."

He shrugged. "I was you, I'd do what you're doing, but I'm gonna have to hurt you.

"You sure as hell better try."

I've heard that our fight is still talked about once in awhile in the neighborhood. We battled each other for more than thirty minutes. I broke Antonelli's aquiline nose five minutes into it, but he came back to close my right eye with a series of hooks and split my eyebrow with a head butt. I had been studying karate at a dojo in Dorchester. After the cut over my left eye, I knew it was only a matter of time before I could no longer see the punches and I'd be put down. Trying to hold off my mounting desperation, I jabbed Antonelli back with a series of lefts, then slid back a step. As he charged in, I turned on the ball of my left foot, spun my body and drove my right leg straight into the center of his chest. The impact lifted him off his feet and into a stack of barrels lining the alley. A barrel handle opened his forehead. Then I was on him, and we rolled onto the sidewalk, pummeling each other.

At some point in the fight, the old mob boss, Vincent Fallon, had come outside to watch and finally sent one of his soldiers, Bennie Guzzo, over to break it up. Guzzo had grabbed me around the neck. Without thinking, I drove the edge of my hand into his groin. At the same instant, Antonelli, blood obscuring his vision, had thrown one of his left hooks. Guzzo was bending forward in pain and caught Antonelli's punch square on his jaw. He toppled into the side of a parked car and slumped to the ground, unconscious. Shocked, we stopped long enough to recognize who we had attacked.

"Holy shit," Antonelli mumbled through swollen lips. "It's Bennie the Crimp."

I had heard of Bennie and his ugly reputation. "Jesus," I muttered. "We're screwed."

Luckily, Vincent Fallon found the inadvertent downing of his muscle funny. He excused the mistake and ordered Antonelli and me to shake hands, calling us "a coupla tough monkeys."

Since that fight, the monkeys had held a grudging respect for each other. But we had kept to our different sides of the street, and different sides of the law.

I hadn't been in Southie for years. I knew what neighborhood Snake lived in, and I finally found the right street when I recognized the one-story brick and concrete building I'd seen in police surveillance photos.

It featured a double garage door and a single door to its right. The single door had a pebbled-glass window on which *O'Hara Auto Repair* was painted in gold script. In reality, cars were of no interest to the occupants unless they were stolen.

I circled the block in search of parking, always in short supply in any part of Boston, and didn't find so much as a crack between the cars lining the street. I finally did what Bostonians do when they can't find a parking spot. I edged the sports car's left tires onto the sidewalk next to the garage and shut off the engine.

I was in luck—O'Hara Auto Repair was open. Frankie Fallon, Antonelli, Tony the Fix, and Ronnie Numbers were playing cards at a table against the far wall. Three wide-bodies sprang to their feet as I entered, blocking my view of the back table. Another, thinner figure appeared on my left. It was Sal Cataldo. He and I had grown up on the same block.

"Hey, Sal. Remember me? Nick Magill."

Cataldo wore a pair of wire-rimmed glasses that almost made him look scholarly, but the eyes behind the lenses had not spent much time reading anything except the racing form. They had seen everything nasty in this world so often that they no longer seemed to blink. Now they examined me as if I was some vaguely familiar species of bug.

"Nicky Magill?" he said, scanning my battered face. "Geez, you look like you been playing Frisbee in the Expressway." He showed small, even teeth in a tight grin.

I smiled. "I've had a hard life, Sal. Right now, I need to speak to Snake."

"And I need to pat you down."

I nodded, lifting my arms. He was quick and thorough. When he was finished, he nodded to the other thugs and stepped around to face me. His eyes focused on my swollen eye. "Cards," he said. "Every weekend. No one interrupts—you know?"

I leaned closer to Cataldo. I could smell cigarettes and stale beer on his breath.

"Sal, you tell Antonelli it's me. You also tell him, he doesn't talk to me right now, he'll be finishing that game inside Cedar Junction."

The prison's name got Cataldo's attention. "You ain't a cop no more, right?"

"That's right, Sal. This isn't about me. Tell Snake it's about the Fox."

Cataldo showed his teeth again. "Sounds like a fucking nature show."

He stared at me for a moment, then turned and moved to Antonelli's shoulder. He whispered. Antonelli's head came up. He stared across the room at me, then said something to the other players, stood, and strolled across the room.

"Nick Magill. You been fighting Lennox Lewis?" He smiled. "You look like hell.

"Very observant," I said tightly. "I need to talk to you outside."

"Not a good idea," Cataldo said. "He's clean, but we haven't checked the street."

The smile stayed on Antonelli's handsome face. "Yeah, Nick, the last time we stepped outside, you did this." He fingered a slight bump in his nose.

"And you parted my eyebrow. Let's cut the shit, Snake. I'm about to do you a favor and I'm not enjoying one second of it."

Antonelli examined me some more, then nodded. "Okay. I love a mystery. Let's you and me go outside, and I'll see if I like the experience any better than the last time."

"I'm sure you will," I muttered. "I won't, but you will."

I turned and we stepped outside.

I told Antonelli the whole story. As I talked, the gangster's face turned ugly, and he swore under his breath. "So, that's it," I said. "Price is not going to be able to send that rabid dog of yours to kill decent people and then disappear to the witness protection program."

Antonelli, who had been examining the skyline, brought his gaze back to me.

"I got a lot to do in the next day or two. That prick Price thinks he's smarter than he is. This is bad, but maybe not fatal."

"I couldn't care less what happens to you and Fallon," I said. "I just want to screw up Price's little deal."

"You have—I can almost guarantee that."

I felt ill, but I nodded.

Antonelli cocked an eyebrow at me. "So, Hanson killed your ex-wife, and you went after him and wound up taking him and Manzi out, huh?" He shook his head. "First, sorry for your loss."

"Save your condolences for someone who wants them."

"Whoa, you're one testy motherfucker, Nick, but you're a credit to the old neighborhood."

"Fuck the old neighborhood, Snake, and fuck you, too. I'm doing this for Diane and Jimmy. Otherwise, I'd let them take you down."

His face darkened, and then he laughed. "Yeah, I can see this is messing you up—else you'd never come here and talk to me like that." He waved his hand. "It's okay.

I get it." He started to turn away, then stopped. "Thanks, Magill. And I know you don't want to hear this, but too bad—I owe you one."

"The hell you do," I said.

Antonelli shrugged. "That's not your decision to make." He pulled open the door and went inside.

CHAPTER 31

I SAT IN THE PORSCHE for ten minutes after Antonelli went inside. I felt drained—and sick about helping these people, yet I had made the decision. Fallon and Antonelli would cover their tracks, and dangerous men would be hunting Jonathan Price. While I believed that Price deserved whatever fate awaited him, I felt no relief or satisfaction in my actions.

In fact, I felt out of control. I had broken the law and totally compromised a federal investigation because I didn't trust the system, but how the hell could anyone trust career-builders like Holbrook? I had known too many of them. All they cared about were convictions. How they got them did not matter. So they were willing to twist the rules to suit their agendas. If innocent people were hurt, so be it. Like all evil men, they believed that the end justified the means.

So I had fouled the process and probably myself. If Antonelli killed Price, I knew I could live with it. But if I were still a cop I would righteously arrest someone who had done what I did.

The headlights of a car pulled me out of my brooding. I suddenly needed to get out of Boston—as far away from any reminder of my years digging through its garbage as possible. I knew my nightmares might still pursue and overrun me, but I did not want to spend another minute in this goddamned neighborhood.

Easing the Porsche off the curb, I found my way back to the Southeast Expressway. I was exhausted—too tired to drive safely back to Rimfield. I headed south, back toward the Cape. Fatigue caught up with me near Plymouth. I turned off at an exit with a motel overlooking the highway and checked in. The first glow of dawn was streaking the sky when I fell onto the bed. I thought of Kin, of how beautiful she was, and sleep took me in less than a minute.

I was on a roof, hidden behind a chimney. Below me, a growling pack of dogs roamed back and forth through an apple orchard. Some of the larger dogs ran from tree to tree, stopping to stand on their hind legs and peer up into the foliage. Foam dripped from their snapping jaws. Their fangs were long and yellowed. The thought of being found by these creatures terrified me. I pressed myself flat on the roof and edged against the chimney until I could feel its heat.

Suddenly, I heard a cry from below. I lifted my head to see a naked man running among the trees, pursued by the howling pack. He sprinted past the smaller trees and pulled himself into the largest tree, scrambling high into its protective foliage. The dogs leaped against the tree, snarling and barking. I could see movement in the upper branches. The man was safely out of their reach.

I relaxed and put my head back down on the rough tar of the roof. I was suddenly exhausted. I closed my eyes and felt my mind sliding comfortably into sleep. At that instant, I was startled awake by a shriek from the orchard. I looked down to see the boughs of the tree begin to shake violently. Apples, knocked loose, showered to the ground, where they turned to small stones. Suddenly, I heard the snap of a branch as loud as a gunshot. Something heavy fell, crashing through the limbs of the tree and landing heavily on the ground. It was the man. The largest dog was on him immediately, seizing his arm in its jaws and snapping its head back and forth. The man's screaming face turned toward me. It was Jonathan Price. I recoiled as our eyes locked. Then the rest of the pack buried him under their frenzied bodies.

I sat upright in the bed, my heart crashing against my chest. My body ached, my mind was a wasp's nest of confusion. I realized I was scanning the room for the dogs. Of course, there were none. They only ran amok in my subconscious. I swung my legs over the side of the bed and fumbled for my watch on the bed table. Nine-thirty a.m. I needed more sleep, but was unwilling to risk a return to that violent orchard.

Forty minutes later, I pulled into Kin's driveway. I didn't want to wake her, but I also didn't want to miss her if she were going out. I sat in my car with the motor idling, half-listening to a Chopin nocturne. I would wait for another hour. I settled back, closed my eyes and allowed myself to be swept up in the surging piano passages of the composer's passion. As physically frail as Chopin had been, his inner strength seemed to be monumental. He focused his energy on his music and transcended the unhealthy reality of his life. I loved his music.

I was caught in the music when I saw a tousled head appear at the porthole in Kin's front door. The door opened and she peered out at me with a puzzled expression. A thick white terrycloth robe made her seem small and vulnerable. I switched off the engine, climbed out of the car, and walked through the warm morning air to her steps.

"I thought I heard a car engine and wondered if—no, hoped—it was you. What are you doing, sitting out here? Are you okay? Come in."

I climbed the steps and moved past her into the apartment. She was rumpled and sleepy, but at that moment, I thought she was the most beautiful woman I had ever seen.

She closed the door behind me. "I was pretty worried about you," she said.

Without thinking, I reached out to her, and she stepped into my arms.

"I'm okay," I whispered into her hair. "I thought I'd take you out to breakfast, but I didn't want to wake you."

She looked up at me, her face softening. "It's too late," she said. "You awakened me long before this morning." Her hand touched my face as I bent down to her.

I was amazed at how incredibly soft her lips felt.

CHAPTER 32

Two DAYS LATER, the official decision came down from Boston Police Department and the FBI: No charges were filed against me in the deaths of Hanson and Manzi. I couldn't help imagining what the judge would do if he knew all that I had set in motion with Antonelli. Agent Holbrook was not in the courtroom, but the result of my meeting with Antonelli was obvious when he marched up to me after court and called me an asshole.

"I can't prove it, but I know you screwed my operation, you bastard. Over two year's worth of work down the crapper."

Dexter Brohanon emerged from a nearby office. The sight of him ended the agent's tirade. Holbrook lowered his voice. "There'll come a time when you'll be sorry for what you've done, Magill. I promise you that."

"Holbrook, the trouble with you is that you think your damned career is worth what Dwayne Hanson did."

"Think what you want, smart-ass, but remember this—if Fallon or his boys take another life, it's on you."

I said nothing. I hoped the sting of his words didn't show in my face.

As Brohanon reached us, Holbrook stepped back.

"Agent Holbrook, do you have something to discuss with my client?"

"Fuck you both," Holbrook snapped and stalked up the hall.

Brohanon frowned at me. "There a problem here, Nick?"

I watched the agent turn down a side corridor. I shook my head. "Just a bad case of PMS."

Brohanon frowned again. "PMS?"

"Poor miserable shithead."

Jimmy Ryerson's funeral was held at a chapel in Cambridge's Mount Auburn Cemetery the following day. There had been no wake. Kin wanted to attend and asked me to go with her.

The weather gods cooperated by unloading a damp, gray overcast day on us. We met Robbie Atkinson on the way in.

"How are you doing, Robbie?" I asked. It was a stupid question, but I didn't know what else to say. I had not saved his best friend. Hell, I hadn't even saved Robbie. He had handled that himself.

"I'm okay, I guess, Mr. Magill. What happened to your face?"

"It looks worse than it is," I said. "By the way, call me Nick. This is Kin."

He smiled and took her hand. "Jimmy used to talk about you. You helped him a lot."

"Thank you," she said, tears welling. "He loved you like a brother."

Robbie nodded. His eyes were wet as well. "I better get inside."

"You all set for your exams?"

"Yes. My advisor set it up. I can take the make-up finals in a week."

"Good luck."

"Thank you." He started to turn away, then paused. "Thank you for trying to help Jimmy, too. I know that you shot the man who murdered him." He glanced to either side, then said softly, "I glad you killed him, you know? I'm glad it was you."

I had no response to that. He nodded and went inside.

"You okay?" Kin asked.

"Sure," I managed. "let's go insi—" I stared as a limo stopped in the drive. Two men who couldn't have looked more like federal agents if they had worn signs jumped out, scanned the people entering, then one of them tapped on the window of the rear door. It swung open and Jonathan Price stepped out. He wore a dove-gray designer suit with a dazzlingly white shirt and a royal blue tie decorated with gold fleur-de-lis.

Kin stared at the expression on my face. "Who—?"

"Price," I muttered.

Jimmy's mother followed Price out of the limo. She wore an expensive black suit over a peach silk blouse. Pearls caressed her neck while their mates, set in gold, decorated small, perfectly formed ears. Her blonde hair, swept up in a French roll, crowned a face that was no stranger to the cosmetic surgeon's knife. The tucks and tweaks had left her with a tight, vaguely surprised expression.

"Jimmy's mother," Kin said.

I nodded. "A study in funeral chic."

The agents hustled them inside. We followed.

The interior of the little church consisted of a short center aisle dividing ten rows of padded benches that faced a small wooden altar. A deep-bronze metal casket gleamed like a dark jewel in the dim light. The room, only half-filled, was hot and stuffy.

I sat with my eyes on the back of Jonathan Price's head. I remembered burying my mother, and it infuriated me to know that the man who had caused Jimmy Ryerson's death had sprung for a top-of-the-line casket. The smug bastard thought he was buying his way out again.

The minister mouthed the usual platitudes about a young man taken from us too soon, then he segued into the mysteries of God's will. Murder and alcoholism never surfaced in his little sermon. We ended with a generic prayer. Price and Jimmy's mother stood and led the exodus to the foyer where the two federal agents positioned them inside the door.

"Why didn't they go outside?" Kin asked. "Is it raining?"

"No," I said. "They don't want their golden goose to get shot."

"Who would shoot him?"

I hadn't told her what I had done. "He's offended his old masters," I remarked as cryptically as I could.

"The mob?"

"Yep." I took her arm. "Let's go pay our respects."

As the line moved us closer to the grieving, dry-eyed couple, Price began glancing at me. Maybe it was my damaged face, but I doubted it. More likely, I had been pointed out to him or he had been shown my picture. The only people who could have done that were the feds. He accepted Kin's condolences, then squared to face me.

"What are you doing here?" he whispered.

"Paying my respects to Jimmy," I replied.

"I know who you are."

"Then we're even."

He started to move toward the couple behind me. I caught his arm. "I hope you have some jam in your pocket," I said, softly.

He turned to me, frowning. "What?"

"Because you're about to be toast."

"Get away fr—"

"All your plans are worth nothing," I continued. "You're going to prison, where Fallon will have you killed."

"You are crazy." He turned to one of the agents. "Doug."

I patted Price on the shoulder. "I hope you'll have as nice a casket," I said.

CHAPTER 33

Kin had decided to take the first two-week block of vacation time in four years. I stayed with her through the funeral, and the hearing, and then we closed her apartment so she could spend the rest of her vacation at my house in Rimfield.

The next six days were the happiest I'd had in years. Kin was a warm, funny, and intuitive woman who actually liked my sculptures. Our lovemaking was slow and passionate.

I felt like a better man, and perhaps because of that I began to hope that this time I wouldn't run for my car keys when I felt closeness develop. This time I'd be able to wait for the intimacy to unfold without thinking about Diane and bolting.

I resolved to stay in the moment, as they said so often at the A.A. meetings I attended with Kin. In fact, I had actually gone to an Al-Anon meeting—only one. It had been interesting. No, that's a cop-out. It was scary—people talking about the alcoholics in their lives. I had said nothing.

Yet each morning this better man felt compelled to scan the *Boston Globe* for some mention of Jonathan

Price. There was none, and I had no way of knowing if he was alive or dead. I tried to let it go, but every day I would open the paper and look again.

On the seventh day, Art Fowler called. After we had exchanged pleasantries, he asked, "You hear about Jonathan Price?"

"No."

"Took off."

"Took off from where?"

"The Feebs had him stashed in one of their safe houses."

"Why the hell would he run?"

Art chuckled. "Well, and this is off the record, apparently the case against Fallon and Antonelli tanked. They could only get a couple of low-level hoods, so the guy in charge—

"Holbrook?" I interrupted.

"Yeah, that dipshit. Anyway, Holbrook decided to salvage as much face as he could by making an example of Price."

"Good news."

"Except the night before they were going to transfer him to a real lock-down, he boogied. Climbed off a second-floor balcony and disappeared into the mist."

"When did all this happen?"

"Two nights ago."

"I didn't see anything in the paper," I said.

"You won't—at least not right away. Holbrook's trying to rope the runaway before he has to go public."

I smiled. "Yeah. That could be a bit of a career-buster."

"Not good on the old resume," Art agreed.

"So tell me, oh wise one, if Holbrook's keeping this under wraps, how the hell do you know about it?"

"Connections, my lad. My wife's sister is married to a fed who hates Holbrook."

"The good news is that that self-serving stuffed shirt Holbrook is in the shit. The bad news is that that murdering bastard Price is loose again."

"True," Art said. "But if I were Price, I'd be more worried about Fallon and Antonelli than the cops. They almost got him once, and you know they'll try again."

I gripped the phone. "Got him once? How?"

"Sniper. Price was home in his bedroom, primping to go out when a bullet killed his full-length mirror."

"Wow."

"I'll say. They estimated the shooter was over a hundred yards away, up in a tree."

"Price has a lot more luck than he deserves."

"Don't worry, Nick. I think it's about to run out."

We said goodbye after he promised to come out with his wife the next weekend. I sat in my studio and wondered how long a pompous elitist like Price could hide.

CHAPTER 34

I WAS IN MY STUDIO finishing the large, mace-like sculpture I had been working on when Diane had called a week and a half ago. It seemed like a year. The final shafts of metal and wood were attached, and I hoisted the piece into an upright position, straining with each yard of the rope through the pulley. The base groaned as the wood shifted against its anchoring station. Slowly, it moved upward until it was almost vertical. I tied it to a cleat on a supporting beam in the studio. Then I stepped away and stared up at the ten-foot mace looming over me. It was impressive and a little frightening. I smiled to myself, satisfied that I had captured what I was trying for. I was about to call Kin to come down and see it when I heard her calling me.

"Nick, come upstairs for a minute. I want to show you something. Quick, before it goes."

I checked the rope's fastening on the cleat and loped up the staircase to the second-floor living room. Kin stood halfway out the slider that opened onto a six-foot balcony. She was looking up and off to the left. She beckoned urgently.

"Quick, quick before it flies away."

I stepped onto the porch and slipped my arm around her.

"Before what flies away?" I asked, kissing her on the cheek.

She pointed to a tall pine tree at the edge of the woods. "Up there, on top of that pine. It's a peregrine falcon, I'm almost positive. See it?"

I stepped to the railing and strained to see where she was pointing.

"No," I said. "Where?"

She gave me a mischievous grin. "Some detective you are." She jabbed me in the ribs and stepped in front of me, extending her arm again. "Pretend you're shooting a rifle and—"

The force with which she slammed into me took us both off our feet. As I hit the slider, I thought she had tripped.

At that instant, I felt a sharp pain in my chest. Instinctively, I touched the hurt. My hand came away covered in blood. As we both tumbled onto the deck, I realized someone had shot us.

A searing pain raked my chest to my back as I tried to sit up. I turned onto my side, then pushed with my feet against the railing. Kin made a low moaning sound as I reached her. The front of her shirt was flooded in blood, the smell of it slowly erasing the soft perfume she wore. Her eyes were barely focused.

"Kin," I stammered. "I—Hang on, I'll get help."

Kin stirred, blinking her eyes and moving her lips. I leaned closer, but couldn't make out her words. She was deep in shock and I knew I had to get to the phone.

As I dragged myself to the slider another shot tore through the railing and punched a dime-sized hole in the glass. Whoever was trying to kill us was still out there. I crawled into the living room when another bullet shattered the handle of the slider, spraying wood and metal chips onto my back.

The pain in my chest was intense, and the front of my sweatshirt was soaked with blood. I hitched myself onto my knees—the effort sent black spots dancing across my vision. I rested my head against the wall until they cleared, then carefully peered outside. A man was running through the woods toward my sculpture field. He wore a baseball cap turned backwards and a khaki jacket. He carried a rifle high against his chest. When he reached the field, he stepped behind one of the sculptures and aimed the rifle at the slider. Within seconds, he was sprinting toward the house, using my own works as cover.

I dragged myself to a standing position and used the wall to hold me up as I moved to the stairs leading down to my studio. There were guns in the room off my gym. If I could get to them before this man reached the house . . . I was on the third step when I fell.

I was exhausted and I lay on the floor, but I wasn't sure why. I hurt—had I been in an accident? The sharp snap and rattle of breaking glass startled me back to my surroundings. I was on the floor of my studio at the foot of the stairs. My head hurt. When I touched it, a stab of pain spread from a swelling wound where I had smacked the floor when I fell. Then I remembered—someone was trying to kill us, and the breaking glass meant that he was in the house. I reached up for the railing, which caused the studio to swim before my eyes. I could feel my consciousness slipping away again. Fear and anger pulled me back. This son-of-a-bitch may have shot us, but he was not going find me lying on the ground like roadkill.

I managed to get my feet under me and started into the small gym. From the far doorway, I heard a thud and saw a shadow on the wall in the office where I kept my rifles. I was too late. The guns were no longer an option. I doubled back into the studio, lurching past my towering sculpture, to the workbench. I seized a hammer and went to meet the shooter.

CHAPTER 35

My breathing sounded like an engine running with a couple of bad plugs. I was hanging onto the thick support beam halfway across the studio when Jonathan Price edged his way through the door. I could see him eyeball my blood-soaked clothes and smile. I was hardly a threat. Aiming the rifle at me, he stepped into the room.

"Well, Magill, nice digs." He raised his eyebrows in mock surprise. "What? No toast jokes? Perhaps this isn't what you expected."

He moved closer. "You have certainly caused me some minor inconveniences. If Agent Holbrook could prove it, he'd send you to prison in my place." He shrugged. "Unfortunately, he tells me he can't, so I decided that before I disappear, I'd make you and the bitch pay."

At the word bitch, I tried to throw a hammer at him left-handed. It clattered to the floor three feet in front of him.

"Oh, you're the gallant type, eh? I don't share your view—although I must admit my greedy, stupid wife has been useful. Each time her mongrel offspring would get drunk and call her, she'd tell me all about it," he sneered.

"She enabled me to pull the strings on Hanson and my federal friends."

"Fuck you," I snarled. "You screwed up enough for the feds to catch you and turn you into their snitch. You'll screw up this big plan, too."

"Really? Well, you won't be around to see it." He smiled and stepped toward me.

"Good," I rasped, "Come closer, you coward. Let's see if you're still tough without the rifle."

I leaned heavily against the pillar and grabbed the rope lashed to the cleat to hold me up. It helped, but as I tried to keep Price talking, I could feel my strength ebbing. The effort of throwing the hammer had almost put me on the floor, but it had succeeded in bringing Price closer. "It's too bad your buddy Holbrook isn't here to enjoy this," I said.

"That fool was so anxious to make his name on Fallon that he didn't intervene when he heard that my charming step-child was gathering evidence of collusion. I told him it was under control, and he bought it. I counted on that." He gestured again with his gun. "It was bad enough I had to marry Jimmy's pathetic mother after I had his father killed, but it was necessary to consolidate my control of the company. It made working with Fallon easier and safer." He paused, then shrugged. "About a year or so ago, some federal computer nerd got lucky and found a mistake in our books. They had me, but I also had them—Holbrook particularly. I offered him Fallon in exchange for no jail time. He promised to place me in their dreary witness protection program. What he didn't know was that I have millions stashed away. When I finish here, I'll pick it up and be long gone."

I spat blood on the floor.

That seemed to offend him more than the hammer. He brought the gun up and fired at me.

The corner of the pillar exploded next to my head just as I pulled the rope from its cleat. As Price racked another shell into his rifle, I tried to step behind the sculpture's support, but my legs rebelled, and I found myself falling forward into the open, less than ten feet from where Price stood.

The impact of my body on the floor shook the room. Price grinned and aimed the rifle again, then paused, frowning, when he heard the whine of rope whizzing through the pulley, followed by a horrible groaning sound behind him. Instinctively, he turned to stare up. In a clear instant of terror he realized what was happening— he had time to scream once.

I lay on my side. I could see Price's body pinned to the floor by the spiny metal points of my toppled sculpture. A dark pool outlined his body. The studio was silent except for my own uneven breathing. After what seemed like hours, I dragged myself to a sitting position, and then I slowly stood up. I staggered across the studio, using chairs and tables as supports. I knew if I went down again, I would never get back up. Hanging on to the exercise equipment, I made my way through the gym, into the office. I dropped into my desk chair and dialed 911.

Kin was upstairs. Using both hands, I pulled myself to my feet and lurched back to the stairs. Using all my remaining strength, I dragged myself up a step at a time until I reached the living room. My chest and back ached. My left arm seemed to have lost its use.

She lay exactly where I had left her. Her face was drawn and waxen, but as I slid down next to her, I could hear shallow breathing. She was still alive. I turned my head and scanned the top of the pine tree, wondering if the falcon she had seen was still there. I was searching when I closed my eyes for a moment. In that brief darkness, I fell into a bottomless pool.

CHAPTER 36

I SWAM UP TO CONSCIOUSNESS in the ambulance and managed to ask about Kin. The EMT stopped writing, shrugged, and said she was taken in another vehicle.

"Relax," he said. "You're going to make it."

"But what about her?"

The EMT didn't answer. I glared at him, then closed my eyes and slid away.

I clawed my way out of the darkness as a doctor was examining me. He was saying something about going to the O.R.

"Shit," I muttered and the trap door opened again.

I awoke with a start. Kin, still in her whites, was turned away from him, doing something with the bank of machines by my bed.

"Kin," I said weakly.

She turned and looked at me. "You're awake, Mr. Magill."

I blinked at the nurse, pretty in her own right with a turned-up Irish nose dusted with a spray of freckles, but she was not Kin. In that instant, I remembered sitting beside Kin's wounded body.

"Sorry," I panted. "I thought . . . you were someone else."

The nurse bent over me. "It's going to be all right, Mr. Magill," she said. "You've been through a lot."

"What about the woman who was with me? Jean McKinnon. Is she okay?"

"She's okay. She was transferred to Mass General."

"Why? What's wrong?"

"I really don't know," she said, patting my arm. "She wasn't my patient." She straightened and smiled. "You have company outside. A police officer. Mr. Fowler's been here for two days."

I managed a smile. "He just needed an excuse to get out of work. Ask him to come in, please, Ms. . . . ?"

"Bridget Collins. I'll get him."

Moments later, Fowler's bear-like form filled the doorway. "Ah, you're awake. I was beginning to the suspect the Rip Van Winkle Syndrome."

I grinned. "Thanks for coming. I would have perked right up if I knew you were out there."

Art came to the side of the bed. We shook hands. "How're you doing, Nick?"

"Worried as hell about Kin." I shrugged. "But I'm alive."

Art nodded. "They tell me she'll be all right, but she's pretty badly hurt."

"The nurse said she's in Boston—Mass General."

"That's right. They moved her this morning."

"After two days?"

He ran his fingers through his curly hair. "Nick, they had to stabilize her first."

I let that sink in. Art pulled a chair close to the bed and sat down. "The locals have been in and out, checking on you. They have some questions, although it's fairly obvious what happened."

I nodded again. By "locals" he meant the local cops.

He leaned closer. "Holbrook has been going nuts, pestering everybody. He claims you should be charged with everything from manslaughter to mass murder. Apparently Price's death has left him sucking wind. Watch out for him, Nick. He'll screw you if he ever gets the chance."

"I'm not surprised. I fucked this one up pretty good."

"What are you talking about?"

"I got Kin hurt, Art. Price shot her because he was after me."

He frowned. "I get that. What's confusing is why he would delay his vanishing act to take a run at you."

"I screwed Price out of his little deal, then rubbed his nose in it even after Holbrook blamed me."

"What the hell did you do?"

"Let's just say that I made sure Price wouldn't get into the witness protection program." I shrugged. "In the process I screwed Holbrook up, too."

Art waved a big hand at me. "Stop right there, wild man. You're my old partner and my best friend. I don't want to know any more. Not right now. When this is all over, we'll sit out on your deck, have some of that great coffee you make, and you can tell me everything, but not right now. What I don't know can't hurt you."

Art Fowler was a good man and I was damned lucky to have him for a friend. "Thanks, Art," I said.

He gave me a tight grin. "So, let's talk Red Sox."

I glanced down at my thickly bandaged chest. "Looks like I'm out for the season," I said.

There had been a medium splash of news in the *Globe* and the *Herald*. Without, of course, any mention of Holbrook, Fallon, or any ongoing criminal investigation. The *Herald* suggested that Jonathan Price blamed me for the death of his stepson, brooded about it, then went off the deep end and attacked me. Jean McKinnon was treated as an almost anonymous casualty. The spin control was so astute that the story wouldn't even have made a good movie-of-the-week. The local authorities treated it as a home invasion and there were no charges filed.

Chauncey "Mac" McInerny, my nearest neighbor, who had visited me in the hospital several times, showed up to drive me home two days later. Mac, a retired surgeon who jogged at least five miles a day, heard the hospital doc give me strict instructions to stay home and rest. With Kin almost two hundred miles away, that was not going to happen.

When we pulled into my drive and parked, Mac turned to me and smiled. "You heard what the doctor said about rest."

"Sure," I said.

He arched a snow-white eyebrow at me. "Just how are you planning to get to Boston to see your lady friend?"

"Huh?"

"Oh, my. The hero plays dumb, and badly," he said.

I smiled. "I plan to drive," I said.

He scratched his beard. "The hero wasn't playing—he is dumb."

"I've got to see her, Mac."

"And Art's not around?"

"No, he had to go back to work."

"In that case, you best ask the crusty old neighbor to drive you."

"Are you sure?"

He patted me on the shoulder. "Nine a.m. tomorrow okay?"

I lumbered onto my porch and went inside. Someone, probably Mac, had replaced the glass in my door that Price had broken. I climbed the stairs to my bedroom and changed into comfortable sweats. I was back in the kitchen making coffee when my phone rang. I grabbed it, hoping it was Kin. I had not been able to reach her since the shooting.

"You don't fool around, do you?" said a deep baritone voice.

"Who is this?"

"Nicky, it's your old neighborhood calling."

"Antonelli?"

"Now I owe you twice."

I hung up in his ear.

CHAPTER 37

AT 8:59 THE NEXT MORNING, there was a knock at my kitchen door. As I walked in from the living room, I could see Mac McInerny's lean silhouette through the door window. I didn't need to see him to know he was there. Mac was the kind of guy who meant exactly nine a.m. when he said nine a.m. I eased my jacket on and opened the door.

Mac was wearing a beat-up felt snap-brim hat—his "city chapeau," as he called it.

"Ready to go?" he asked.

"Sure am," I replied. I stepped outside and closed the door behind me. We left my porch, climbed into his ten-year-old Mercedes sedan and headed for Boston.

The truth was that I was more than a little apprehensive. I had still not spoken with Kin. Last night, I found that she had been transferred from intensive care to a private room. When I dialed that number, the woman who answered had identified herself as Kin's mother, just in from California. She told me that Kin was sedated and asleep. When I told her of my plan to visit today, she hesitated before saying that Kin had tests scheduled and might not be available.

The fact that she had contacted her mother but had sent me no message seemed a bad omen. Her mother's hesitancy upon hearing my name heightened that ominous feeling. I knew that my actions had placed her directly in harm's way, and that the emotional and physical costs of her injuries were my fault. That would be hard to forgive. Still, I needed to see her, if only to admit responsibility.

Our ride in was uneventful. We talked about running, an activity we sometimes did together. He told me about a new hill route he had found that "would give a mountain goat a workout." I promised to run it with him after I had healed. He dropped me at the Mass General entrance, then looped into the parking garage. We planned to meet in the coffee shop in an hour.

I got directions to her room from the information desk, then waited in a knot of people for the elevator. We all squeezed inside, calling out floor numbers to the person closest to the control buttons. We stopped at every floor. I've been calm in the face of men with guns, aggressive defense attorneys—all sorts of stressful situations. But by the time we had crawled from the first to the eighth floor, a cold finger of sweat tickled my back, and I was wiping my clammy hands on my pant legs.

I followed the busy corridor to room 203. The door was ajar. I took a deep breath and eased it open. The bed was empty, but a woman sat in a chair near the foot of the bed reading a magazine. When she looked up, I was shocked to see a version of Kin twenty years older, but still beautiful.

"Mrs. McKinnon?" I asked.

She nodded, as she stood up and placed the magazine on the bed.

"I'm Nick Magill. We spoke on the phone last evening."

She nodded again. "Hello, Mr. Magill."

"Please. Call me Nick. How is Kin?"

She frowned, then smiled. "Sometimes I forget that Jean has a nickname."

"How is she?"

"I'm Margaret. Pretty badly hurt, I'm afraid. They took her for more X-rays," she glanced at her watch. "Almost a half-hour ago."

"Do you mind if I wait?"

"I guess that would be all right. It's not visiting hours yet, but . . ."

"I was driven here," I said. "My friend is waiting downstairs."

She nodded. "It's all right, I guess." She pointed at her chair. "I see you were hurt, too. Would you like to sit down? I'm afraid there's only one chair."

I opted to stand and we waited in silence for almost five minutes. Finally I asked her about Kin growing up in Coronado. She smiled and recounted stories of her little girl's happy childhood, which were much more joyful and carefree than Kin's versions.

I remembered my mother's romanticized portrayal of my deceased father. Her reconstructions of our family life had always angered me, but since they usually came in the form of letters, I had time to cool off, so as not to torpedo her fantasies in person. It was strange how my mom needed to cleanse our history so her memory would not have a cutting edge—even though this fiction left festering pockets of pain for all of us.

"Jean has talked about you," she said, returning us both to the present. She smiled ruefully. "Of course, she hasn't given me many details. How long were you together?"

Her gaze did not meet mine as she asked the question. Perhaps she disapproved of us being together at my house.

Then I realized that she was uncomfortable because her daughter did not confide in her.

"A short time," I said slowly. "Less than a month."

I stared at Margaret McKinnon's averted face. I remembered Kin's stories about her brutal father, and I wanted to ask this woman why she hadn't taken better care of her children. But Kin was in the hospital because of me, so who the hell was I to ask that question?

"Nick."

I turned to see Kin, her shoulder and arm heavily bandaged, being wheeled into the room. I went to her and leaned down to kiss her. She gave me her cheek.

The nurse helped her into the bed. Kin thanked her, then turned to her mother. "Mom, would you mind giving Nick and me a few minutes alone?"

"All right," her mother said. "Should I—Do you need anything?"

"Some new magazines would be nice. Thank you."

Her mother glanced at me, then hurried out.

"Sit down," Kin said. Her face was thinner and pale. Fatigue smudged her eyes. Her hair, pinned up, looked disheveled, with strands hanging down beside her face. She was still beautiful.

"Thanks. How are you?" I asked.

Her lips twisted into a faint smile. "Not so good," she said. "At first, they thought I might lose my arm altogether, or the use of it. Now they think that with physical therapy and time . . ." She left it at that.

"I am so sorry," I said.

"You didn't shoot me, Nick. Look, you're hurt yourself."

"Your body slowed the bullet. I'm all right."

"It's not your fault."

"My actions brought Price there."

She was silent for a moment. Then, taking a deep breath, she said, "I'm going back to California for long-term treatment. There's an excellent physical therapy program in San Diego."

I looked at her, but said nothing.

"I'm sorry," she said. "But when my Mom flew here, it made me realize that I have some amends to make to her."

"Amends?"

"Like owning my part of what happened between us. It wasn't all her fault. I do love her, you know?"

I nodded. "There are excellent programs here, as well."

"I know, but I'm not staying."

"Because of me?"

She frowned. "In part. You know that I really do care about you. I know that may not be apparent since I haven't contacted you at all, but it's true. I just needed time to think."

"About what?"

"The violence, I guess. I know you were doing what you had to do, and I made the decision to tag along, but . . ." Tears welled in her eyes. "God, it was awful. All of it—Manzi and that monster Hanson, poor Jimmy, and then that man Price." She fluttered her good hand. "There's too much trauma here."

"Trauma that I brought into your life."

She shrugged, then winced. "Jimmy was the instigator. He started the events that killed Diane and all the rest." She smiled at me. "You were the one who stopped the bad guys. I just happened to get in the way."

"I can fly out. Help you with therapy."

She shook her head. "No. I'm sorry, but I need some time away from any extra reminders of what happened."

I nodded. My wounded chest began to throb. "Is there anything I can do?"

"Remember me kindly in your prayers."

"I could think of you in no other way," I said. "You saved my life."

"You mean the shooting?"

I stood up. "No. I mean my emotional life. You enabled me to love again."

Tears began to roll down her cheeks. "But I'm leaving you, like Diane did."

"No, it's different." I thumbed some moisture from my eyes. "She froze my heart. You thawed it out."

Time and sound seemed to freeze as we looked at each other through blurry eyes. Finally, when I couldn't stand it any more, I leaned over her. She tipped her face to mine and we kissed, briefly and sweetly. Then I got the hell out of there.

CHAPTER 38

Tᴇɴ ᴅᴀʏs ʟᴀᴛᴇʀ, I sat in my living room at eleven p.m. and stared out at the sculptures in my floodlit field. Yesterday, after I had summoned the stamina to hose the remains of Jonathan Price off of the broken sculpture, Mac McInerny had jogged the two miles to my house and helped me to hoist the piece back into its upright position. I appreciated Mac's neighborliness but discouraged any unnecessary conversation. After a few minutes, he got the idea and left, but not before I had again agreed to go for a run as soon as I felt ready.

Afterwards, I sat in my studio and thought about repairing the tines broken when the mace had fallen on Price. But, as usual, all I was able to do was sit, trapped in the chair, as if all my power had been drained away. For the past week, the prospect of doing any significant work seemed beyond reach.

After it became obvious that no artistic breakthrough was in the cards, I left the studio, made some coffee, and went upstairs to the living room where I'd spent most of my time since the shooting, thinking.

The events in the last month were drenched in irony. When she called me, Diane had inadvertently started the process that freed me from the prison of our break-up. Kin was the one who finally found the key that unlocked my cell, but I lost her because I had underestimated the man behind all this and put her in danger. At the moment when I knew Kin and her mother were walking through security at Logan, I felt a horrible loss and yet . . . somehow I also knew that the release she had provided me would not end with her departure. Outside, everything looked the same. Inside, everything was changing.

I stood and switched off the field lights. The movement caused my chest to throb. The wound was healing nicely, according to the docs, but a dull ache still hung around to aggravate me. I didn't mind, though—whenever I thought of Kin, I knew her pain shrank mine to the level of an itch.

A flash of lightning in the distance, followed by the rumble of thunder, caught my attention. A mountain storm was building fast and moving this way. I climbed the stairs to the loft hallway that ran past my bedroom. At the end of the hall, a ladder reached up into the hexagonal cupola that sat atop my house. Ignoring the twinges of pain, I climbed up to the small room. The storm was almost on me as I opened one of the windows in the stuffy space, then lowered myself into an old leather chair. Illuminated by the lightning, my sculptures became misshapen sentinels, guarding my domain.

I now knew that this house I built had become my prison. Too often, I had hidden in it from the outside world and from my own heart. I had even built these wooden and metal statues to stand guard. Now, all that was about to change. I had made some stupid mistakes since Diane's death, but I had taken action. That action had led me to Kin, and she had opened a door that I had to walk through, if only to honor her. I had no idea where all this would lead. I only knew that it would not be boring. I trusted that my sculpting would begin again, but so would something else.

The wind swung around and began to whip rain through the open window and across my body. I made no effort to shield myself. Then the storm was upon me, roaring, shaking my tiny perch. As its energy coursed through my body and mind, I leaned forward and yelled into its mindless force, "I'm back!"

CPSIA information can be obtained
at www.ICGtesting.com
Printed in the USA
LVHW021217251121
704321LV00002B/195

9 781935 052777